BANNER YEAR

BANNER
Y · E · A · R

BETTY CAVANNA

Troll Associates

Poetry excerpts are from *The Poetry of Robert Frost,* edited by
Edward Connery Lathem. Copyright 1923, © 1969 by Holt,
Rinehart and Winston. Copyright 1936, 1951 by Robert Frost.
Copyright © 1964 by Lesley Frost Ballentine. Reprinted by
permission of Henry Holt and Company.

A TROLL BOOK, published by Troll Associates,
Mahwah, NJ 07430

Published by arrangement with William Morrow and Company, Inc.
For information address William Morrow and Company, Inc.,
105 Madison Avenue, New York, New York 10016.

First Troll Printing, 1988

Printed in the United States of America.

10 9 8 7 6 5 4 3 2 1

ISBN 0-8167-1265-4

FOR ELEANOR DICKSON

CHAPTER
1

AT A TIME WHEN MOST of her friends at school were
falling in love with boys, Cindy found herself falling in love with a horse. His name was Banner, a
bold, bright name for a glossy black pony standing
just fourteen hands.

Banner was boarding at Heatherfield Farm,
where Cindy first saw him on a cool October day,
when his mane was blowing in an offshore breeze
and the heart-shaped white mark on his forehead
appeared clearly against his ebony coat.

There was a showy palomino in the pasture, a
frisky chestnut mare, and a big, strong roan, but it

was the black pony that made her heart turn over when he came trotting up to the fence and amiably accepted a handful of grass from her hand.

Wide-set and intelligent, his eyes were his most remarkable feature. He looked at her appraisingly as he munched the grass, then turned away and frisked along the fence line, tossing his mane, showing off. Obeying some mysterious impulse, he stopped abruptly, turned his head to regard the stranger for several seconds, and started back.

Cindy waited. Intuitively she felt that the pony was inviting her to speak, to greet him, to recognize their spontaneous rapport. Delight flooded through her. She had known other horses, some far more handsome than this animal, with his compact body and compelling eyes, but none with such instant appeal.

Slowly the pony returned to stand before her. Cindy rested her elbows on the top rail of the fence and stretched out a hand in welcome. As she felt his cool lips nuzzling her palm, she was conscious of a strange, exciting, inward lurch. "Hello," she said, speaking softly. "Hello, beautiful."

"He certainly has a beautiful disposition," said a tall, rangy woman wearing duck boots and patched jeans, who had come so silently along the rutted lane that Cindy turned in surprise. She looked up into a weather-beaten face that seemed older than the direct gray eyes studying her.

Cindy ventured, "Are you . . . the owner?"

"Of the farm, yes. Of the horse, no. Banner is a boarder. My name is Helen Park. And yours?"

"Cynthia Foster. People call me Cindy." After the staccato sound of Mrs. Park's voice she felt that she was speaking unusually slowly. "I'm one of the 4-H girls who signed up to look after the horses."

"You live near here?"

"About a mile away. Heatherfield Farm is an easy bike ride from Strawberry Hill Road."

Mrs. Park nodded. "Have you worked much with horses?"

"Some," Cindy replied cautiously. "I've taken riding lessons since I was eleven years old, whenever I could earn the money. After class I used to hang around the stable."

"Good. You learn things that way."

Mrs. Park's approval induced a confidence. "I like to be around horses, and I love to ride." Cindy's brown eyes sparkled at the mere thought.

"Well, you'll get in some riding here. After work, mind you. It's not all fun and games. Mucking out stalls and hauling sacks of feed and bedding are heavy going." As she spoke, Mrs. Park's eyes inspected Cindy's slender frame.

"I'm stronger than I look," Cindy assured her.

Mrs. Park turned away, her attention caught by a trio of girls standing on the brow of the hill near the barn. "Come along," she said in her quick, clipped manner, and started up the lane with an easy stride.

Cindy managed to keep pace, although she kept looking over her shoulder at the black pony. "Who does Banner belong to?" she asked after a moment.

"Laurel Proctor. A girl from up-island," said Mrs. Park. "You may know her."

"Just by sight," Cindy replied. "She was a senior last year when I was only a freshman." The image that appeared in Cindy's mind was of a willowy girl with long copper-colored hair who moved through the corridors of the high school with an air of self-confidence.

"Why does she want to board Banner out?" Cindy's brown eyes widened uneasily. "Doesn't she like him?" She was sure if she owned the black pony, she would never let him go.

"Oh, Laurel loves him," replied Mrs. Park. "She comes to see him whenever she can, but she's studying nursing in Boston. No part-time proposition!"

Boston? So far away! No wonder Laurel couldn't get back to the island often. For a little while, Cindy thought, I can pretend Banner is mine. Then she chided herself for such childishness. She had just turned sixteen, was a sophomore in high school, and daydreaming was no longer the pleasure it had been in grammar school.

Mrs. Park was waving to the girls on the hill, all

three of them classmates of Cindy's. Hope and Faith Bowman were twin sisters who lived in Oak Bluffs, and Caroline Treat was her best friend and next-door neighbor. Caroline was as fair as Cindy was dark. She had blue eyes and the wispy strawberry blond hair that so often seemed to go with freckles, but her skin was creamy and unblemished. The girls had known each other since kindergarten days and shared the distinction of having been born on Martha's Vineyard. "The two C.'s," their friends had called them, because they were always together.

Caroline took a tentative step toward Cindy now. Next to the square, sturdy twins she seemed unexpectedly fragile. Although Cindy knew her appearance was deceptive, that she could run like a gazelle, play a fast game of tennis, and had a light seat on horseback, she wondered if she had been wrong in persuading her to join this program.

Mrs. Park greeted each of the girls in a businesslike manner. "Our barn doubles as a stable," she said, and led them through an open door to rows of stalls ranged at right angles against two walls. Only a couple were occupied, since most of the horses were out in the fields on this clear afternoon, so after a quick tour she gathered the girls and outlined the duties of the 4-H team. Even to Cindy these seemed considerable.

Each girl was expected to spend two hours every weekday at the farm, cleaning stalls, spreading lime and fresh shavings, grooming the horses, washing buckets, caring for tack, then riding for an hour, if possible.

Caroline didn't consider it possible. She rolled her eyes at Cindy and groaned audibly.

Mrs. Park was too absorbed to notice. "I'll post a time chart on the wall over here," she said, "and see how you make out the first week. Don't be concerned. We'll adjust it if necessary."

The twins regarded Mrs. Park stoically, but Caroline whispered to Cindy, "Sounds like a lot more work than I thought."

Shrugging, Cindy whispered back, "It's a good thing I decided not to go out for girls' soccer." She realized it was also fortunate, from Caroline's point of view, that the tennis season was almost over.

"I've been promised six helpers in this group," Mrs. Park continued. "Of course, you'll take turns with the morning feeding."

"Morning?" squealed Caroline. "Before school?"

Mrs. Park's gray eyes glinted with controlled amusement. "Horses have to have breakfast."

"At what time?" Caroline groaned.

"Between six and six-thirty."

Caroline groaned again, with more emphasis.

Mrs. Park laughed, making a sound like a donkey's bray. "Is it such a big deal to get up once a week at five o'clock in the morning?"

"I don't mind," said Cindy. Just to be in a stable was pure joy, and she anticipated with pleasure the chores Caroline dreaded.

"It's not like it was every day," said Faith Bowman comfortingly.

Caroline managed a smile and a shrug. "I'd better find something louder than a Mickey Mouse alarm clock."

"Now for the good news," Mrs. Park said. "After you become acquainted with the farm, each of you will be assigned a horse that will be in your special care. Doesn't that appeal to you?"

It certainly appealed to Cindy, because it was as close as she might ever come to having a horse of her own. If only it could be Banner! To be put in charge of the black pony, to be able to take him on daily rides—what great fun! She started daydreaming again until Mrs. Park used a phrase strange to her. "therapeutic equitation."

"That's a fancy way of saying we're going to teach handicapped children to ride horseback, and as you girls know, you're part of the program. We train the horses to be steady and patient with kids who are timid or frightened. Some of them have never been close to a horse before. It will be quite a challenge."

"Can they all actually learn to ride?" asked Caroline curiously.

"No. Some can be taught only to sit on a horse. But mastering their fear of such large animals helps develop their self-esteem."

"Don't the horses get scared of the kids?" Hope Bowman questioned.

"Not if we've done a good job and the horse is ready for the program. We keep about fourteen horses here. Some are too high-strung to work with these children. A few are borderline. Come on down to the pasture with me and meet Flax. She's lovely to look at, but watch out! She can behave like a witch on occasion."

While the others were being introduced to the palomino mare whose foibles were so unpredictable, Cindy's attention again became focused on Banner. She noticed that below the heart on his forehead he had an odd marking down near his upper lip. At first she thought it was a scar, then realized that white and gray hair had grown in an uneven patch that looked remarkably like a map of the island.

Mrs. Park finished with her description of the palomino's problems. Then she also turned her attention to Banner, who was nuzzling Cindy's outstretched hand. "Take a look at this pony. He wasn't always so gentlemanly. In fact, he was a young hellion when Laurel Proctor first owned him.

Now he's a perfect lamb with the handicapped kids. Last year he was their favorite, and no wonder!"

"Why do you call him a pony?" asked Hope Bowman. "He's not little."

"A pony is a horse not exceeding fourteen-point-two hands," Mrs. Park explained. "Banner comes under the limit."

In the days of her riding lessons, Cindy had learned that the height of horses was measured in hands, but she was sure Hope hadn't the slightest idea what Mrs. Park was talking about. The group started to straggle up the hill again, Cindy and Caroline bringing up the rear.

"You're just as crazy about horses as ever, aren't you?" Caroline asked pensively.

Cindy nodded. "Aren't you?"

"Not really. I think for me they were a phase. I still like to ride, though."

"Remember when we first took lessons, back in fifth grade?" Cindy mused. "They kept riding us around and around the ring forever!"

Caroline nodded. "When we were just dying to get out in the woods on our own."

"We finally made it," recalled Cindy with a grin. "Then I didn't notice a low tree branch and landed in the sand on the bridle path!"

"I was so scared," Caroline confessed. "You couldn't talk. You could only squeak."

"I had the wind knocked out of me," Cindy admitted, "but it didn't matter. I loved every minute of every ride. I'd still rather be on horseback than anywhere else."

"I remember all those horse books you got me to read. *The Black Stallion, Misty of Chincoteague, The Red Pony.*"

Cindy smiled. "*Misty* was the best. *The Black Stallion* was a boy's book, and *The Red Pony* was too hard for us." Cindy had also read Marguerite Henry's story called *Justin Morgan Had a Horse.* When they caught up with the rest of the group, this induced her to blurt out a question about Banner's breeding.

"Could he possibly be a Morgan, Mrs. Park?"

"If that's a guess, it's a good one, Cindy," Mrs. Park replied with a chuckle. "He's part Morgan, part mystery. At least that's what Laurel and I tell people."

Part Morgan. The news warmed Cindy's heart. At once she attributed to Banner all the qualities of the "big-little" horses Marguerite Henry had so admired. No wonder it had been love at first sight!

The afternoon light was waning, coloring the autumn fields with tones of red and purple as subtle as those found in old oriental rugs, but Cindy was oblivious to their beauty. She turned and looked back at the lower pasture, where Banner was trotting toward a far corner. Flax was standing there under a group of birches dressed in golden leaves.

"Looks like a picture, doesn't she?" Caroline asked.

"She?"

"Flax."

"Oh." Cindy had eyes only for Banner. The honey-colored mare didn't appeal to her.

"We'd better be getting along," suggested Caroline. Together the two girls said good-bye to Mrs. Park and started toward the shed where they had left their bicycles.

Cindy walked sedately, although she felt like leaping into the air and shouting for joy. She was happier than she had been since the start of school in September. Banner was going to make a big difference in her life!

Side by side the girls wheeled their bicycles along the rutted lane leading to Lagoon Road. A Boston plane flew overhead, leaving a contrail like a thin cloud in the fading sky. As she watched it, Cindy had an unsettling thought that she turned into a question. "Do you think I dare ask to be assigned to Banner?"

"Banner?" If she had heard the name, Caroline had forgotten.

"The black pony, Caro. Wake up!"

Her eyes squinting against the sunset's sudden

blaze, Caroline considered. "I wouldn't if I were you. It's not your right to suggest what Mrs. Park should do."

This was probably good advice, Cindy realized. She remembered her mother once saying, "Caroline's very perceptive. She's growing up fast while you're still a tomboy."

Cindy was no longer a tomboy. Having preferred playing with boys all through her childhood, she had changed since she entered high school. Now she actually avoided the boys she had known so well. They had changed, too.

Once on the macadam, it was safer to ride single file. Caroline went ahead, and Cindy followed, pondering these changes. Not only had the boys altered their attitude toward girls along with the timbre of their voices, but most of them acted as though they had never been playmates. They either ignored her or treated her with a kind of arrogance she didn't understand. Sometimes they teased Caroline, who seemed to enjoy it and bridled prettily, but they never teased Cindy, not even when they went out on occasional group dates. When couples held hands or leaned together, whispering, in the movies, Cindy could feel herself stiffen in embarrassment. She had known all these boys since first grade, and none of them attracted her except as friends.

The interior of the island was hilly, and after

pedaling for half a mile, Caroline slipped off the seat of her bike and began to walk once more. Cindy joined her at a point where they could look down at the water, flat and shiny now that the offshore breeze had died. Looking back, she could see Nantucket Sound in the distance where the lagoon communicated with the sea. Only a single white sail showed on this early evening. Peace had descended on the Vineyard with the departure of the last of the summer visitors. No impatient motorists, just an occasional car or pickup truck passed along the road.

"Nice out, isn't it?" asked Caroline idly.

"Nice," Cindy agreed.

"Do you know that Johnny Trumbull thinks he's made the football squad?"

Since Johnny and football were the farthest things from Cindy's mind, she shook her head.

"Haven't you noticed how much he's grown over the summer?"

"No."

"He's almost six feet, and he's gained weight, too. He hopes to play varsity fullback next year," Caroline said.

"Really?"

"You don't sound interested. Where's your school spirit?" Caroline was smiling, although she sounded annoyed.

"Sorry. I wasn't really listening," Cindy said apologetically.

After a couple of minutes Caroline tried a different tack. "Who else has signed up for work at Heatherfield Farm? Do you know?"

"Haven't a clue," replied Cindy. They had reached a brow of the hill, so she got on her bike again and coasted off ahead, close to the edge of the macadam.

"Do you think you'll like working there?" Caroline shouted.

"I'm sure I will!" Cindy shouted back, turning her head for a second. "Cheer up, Caro! We'll have a marvelous time."

The girls didn't talk again until they turned into Strawberry Hill Road and reached the short drive leading to Caroline's house. Lights were being turned on inside as the Treats' golden retriever came across a stretch of grass with his tail wagging in greeting. As always, Cindy was struck by the orderliness of the place in contrast with her own house only a few hundred yards away. Although her father worked as a contractor—and in hard times as a carpenter—he never seemed to find time to repair the front steps, patch the roof, or prune the bushes. Nevertheless, Cindy loved him dearly. He had a pleasant, easygoing disposition, whereas Mr. Treat tended to be impatient and overly precise.

As usual, Cindy stopped for a moment to say

good night, braking her bicycle on the gravel and mentioning that she would have to get some rubber boots before she started work at the farm.

Caroline glanced down at her own shoes. As though she could read Cindy's thoughts, she asked, "What do they call that footgear Mrs. Park was wearing—muck boots?"

"That's near enough," Cindy said with a laugh as she inched a pedal forward. "Bye now. See you on the bus."

Caroline, however, wasn't quite ready to let Cindy go. "I've been thinking about the kids we're going to be working with," she said. "The twins are all right, I guess, and of course you're great, but I hope there are going to be a couple of boys."

Cindy looked at her friend in puzzlement. Her thoughts had been so concentrated on Banner that Caroline's concern surprised her. What difference did it make whom they worked with? Only the horses—especially the black pony—interested her. But as she looked at the expression in Caroline's mild blue eyes, she knew she could never explain how she felt. "Boys?" she asked blankly.

"Of course. Boys."

"Who needs boys?" Cindy muttered to herself as she pedaled away.

CHAPTER

2

HER MOTHER WAS SETTING the table for dinner when Cindy bounced into the house. "You're late, dear," she said mildly.

"I know." Taking knives, forks, and spoons from her mother's hand, Cindy began to help. Her eyes were bright with memories; her hair was a tumble of short brown curls, looking almost black in contrast with her clear, faintly tanned skin. "Oh, Mom, I had the most wonderful day."

"Don't tell me you got an A in algebra."

Cindy discounted the remark with a chuckle. "Remember the 4-H horse program I decided to join? Well, we went to Heatherfield Farm this afternoon and met the owner, Mrs. Park. You may know her."

"Slightly. Tall, thin, wears her hair down her back in a thick braid."

"I didn't notice her hair, but there's this horse, Mom. His name is Banner. . . ."

Cindy launched into a description of her meeting with the black pony. As she put glasses on the table, poured milk for her brother, Peter, and distributed napkins, she kept talking. Her mother had been her first and most satisfactory confidante. Although there were a few things they didn't discuss, on most subjects Cindy was as easy and frank with her as with a close friend her own age.

Mrs. Foster stirred the beef stew simmering on the stove, peeled a garlic clove for the salad dressing she then whipped with a fork, and listened. She was well aware of Cindy's enthusiasm for horses and glad that she would get some practical training in their care. Still, it was a lot of work to take on outside school hours. "Do you think you can handle it, darling?" she asked. "And keep up your grades as well?"

Cindy frowned. "I'll do my best." Privately she thought, So what if I'm not in the top tenth percentile? She knew the stress her mother put on education, but there were other things just as important, weren't there?

Peter came into the kitchen carrying a gray kitten that had wandered up the back steps the night before. Nearly ten years old now, he was growing taller and thinning out. In a troubled manner he asked, "Have you decided yet? Can I keep him, Mom?"

Mrs. Foster pushed a wisp of long hair back into place in a casual twist and sighed. The dark green eyes that were her chief distinction focused briefly on her son. "I think we'd better discuss it with your father," she said gently. "We can't keep every stray the summer people leave behind." Indeed, as Cindy and her mother both knew, the SPCA kennels were crowded with abandoned animals. Unless homes could be found for them, they inevitably would be destroyed.

"I'll take good care of him," Peter promised.

"For the first few days," Mrs. Foster predicted.

"No. Honestly! I'm growing up, Mom. You keep saying it's time I took some responsibility."

Cindy went over and stroked the kitten's soft fur. "Does he have a name?"

"I call him Silver."

"Heigh-ho, Silver," Mrs. Foster murmured reminiscently. She was stirring the stew again and looking at the clock. "Your father's late, too," she said to Cindy.

At that moment the sound of a pickup truck

could be heard in the yard, making the usual complaining rattle and squawk when parked abruptly. "There's Jim now," said Mrs. Foster, and began pouring French dressing over the salad greens.

"Mm, smells good in here." Jim Foster walked over to the counter to kiss his wife lightly on the cheek. "Looks good, too," he added as he glanced at the big round table in the kitchen window embrasure that looked out toward a blur of pine woods. He was speaking, Cindy knew, of the centerpiece, a frothy arrangement of the last of the wild purple asters.

Mrs. Foster smiled appreciatively. "We'll have to make do with greens from now on, I'm afraid." While her husband went to wash up, she ladled the stew into a big tureen, took toasted rolls out of the oven, and told Peter to scrub his hands after handling the kitten.

Meanwhile, Cindy's thoughts returned to Banner. She ate abstractedly, unaware of the family conversation until Peter's yip of delight brought her back to the present. He ran around the table and hugged his father. "I promise," he cried. "And if Silver gets fleas, I'll give him a bath!"

"Cindy, tell your father about your afternoon at the farm," her mother suggested after a while.

Willingly she told him about the horses, but she didn't single out Banner. There were lines of fatigue in her father's face, and he seemed to be listening with more patience than interest. When he stifled a yawn, she broke off.

Later, while she was doing her homework, Cindy herself started to yawn. After such an exciting day reaction set in, and she closed her books and went off to bed earlier than usual, setting her alarm clock for six o'clock. Might as well get in practice, she reasoned, for the days when she would be getting up even earlier to feed the horses at Heatherfield. In the morning she finished her homework in a burst of concentration and was early for the school bus.

Caroline ran up to the bus stop at the last minute, raking a comb through her fluffy hair as she climbed the steps. "Whoo," she breathed as she skidded to the empty seat beside Cindy. "Just made it." Then, in a confidential whisper, she said, "Guess what? Johnny Trumbull phoned last night! He asked me for a date."

"Well," said Cindy, nonplussed as to how to reply. "Well, that's nice." Having known Johnny since preschool days, she had always considered him rather truculent and nobody to get excited about.

"Nice? I think it's wonderful!" Caroline's eyes were starry, although she was still out of breath.

"For when?" asked Cindy.

"Saturday night," replied Caroline proudly. "It's a double date, actually, with Tracy Jones and Dick Perry. We're going over to Tracy's house to watch videos of old movies."

"Well, that'll be fun," said Cindy. Although neither of the boys appealed to her, she felt a small twinge of envy. As a matter of fact, she couldn't think of a single boy in the sophomore class she yearned to go out with. There were a couple of juniors she admired, but she felt that they were beyond her reach.

"I can't decide what to wear," Caroline was saying. "Everything in my closet looks so tacky, but I doubt that Mom will spring for something new."

Since Cindy thought exclusively in terms of jeans or pants, she wasn't much help, although she tried to react sympathetically. "You have lots of pretty clothes, Caro!"

"Then come over after school and help me choose!"

"I can't today," said Cindy.

"Why not?"

"Because I'm going to the farm to see if Mrs. Park has posted the assignments," Cindy admitted.

"You and your horses!" Caroline's voice rose in annoyance. "Can't you ever think of anything else?"

"Boys, you mean?" Cindy allowed herself to

sound faintly contemptuous and turned her head, pretending to stifle a yawn.

"Oh, act your age!" Caroline scolded. "After all, we're sixteen."

"None of the boys in our class turns me on," Cindy said with a shrug, then added plaintively, "Why are you so anxious to grow up? Things are great just as they are." Then, trying to fend off a quarrel, she suggested, "Why don't I stop by on my way home after I leave Heatherfield?"

"Okay," Caroline agreed grumpily, and spent the rest of the ride looking out the window at the cloud-strewn sky. Cindy opened her English book and stared down at a page without reading it. She wondered why they were scrapping when they had managed always to get along so well.

However, in the alternate bustle and boredom of an unremarkable school day, the conversation was forgotten. Cindy made an earlier bus than Caroline and hurried into the house to drop off her books and pick up her bicycle. She met her mother about to take Peter for a dentist appointment in Edgartown. When Cindy said she was headed for the farm, Mrs. Foster said, "Fine. You'll be close enough to Oak Bluffs to run an errand. Your father needs a ticket picked up from the Steamship Authority. He's taking the truck to Cape Cod Saturday to bring back some building materials."

Cindy was willing enough, although it would

double the length of her ride. She started off in a light drizzle, her raingear stowed in the bicycle basket. By the time she reached the farm, however, the sun was trying to break through the clouds.

The barn door was wide open, but Mrs. Park was nowhere to be seen, nor was there an assignment schedule posted on the inside wall. Three horses were in their stalls, but the others apparently had been turned out to pasture in spite of the threat of rain. Cindy hurried down the hilly path and found the palomino and a big gray gelding in the lower field, but there was no sign of Banner.

Disappointed, Cindy sat on the top rail of the fence and chewed a blade of grass until a distant whinny alerted her to a horse and rider emerging from a woodland bridle path in the distance. A few minutes later Mrs. Park came trotting up the lane on Banner's back, reining in when she encountered Cindy. "You're scheduled to be here tomorrow, not today," she said in surprise.

"I know." Cindy flushed, not wanting to admit her real purpose. "I was going to Oak Bluffs on an errand and just thought I'd stop by."

Mrs. Park accepted the explanation without comment. "Since you're here, how about getting up on Banner? You can take him around the paddock and let me watch you ride."

"He won't object to a stranger?" asked Cindy, controlling her eagerness.

"Not this lad." Mrs. Park leaned forward and stroked the pony's neck.

She turned Banner's head toward the nearby paddock, and Cindy followed, opening the gate and closing it after they were inside. Mrs. Park slid off the pony's back and handed the reins to Cindy beside a mounting block, saying, "Don't tire him. He's had a good workout already."

Lightly Cindy swung herself into the saddle. The pony was small enough to make her feel secure in her knee grip, with a compact back easy to straddle comfortably and a quiet stance until she signaled a walk, then a trot. They circled the enclosure once while Mrs. Park looked on. Then Cindy put Banner into an easy rocking-chair canter, and he responded with an alacrity that warmed her very soul.

Mrs. Park smiled and nodded her head, although horse and rider were oblivious to her unspoken praise. Never had Cindy felt more attuned to a mount. She and Banner shared a marvelous affinity, a sort of preknowledge of how each would move, a lovely closeness. Cindy took a long breath of sheer delight, aware of Banner's slightly sweaty, horsey smell. He smelled good, and he felt good. She could have cantered on forever, but obedient to her instructions, she eased him back to a walk.

"If you work as well as you ride, you'll be an asset to the program," Mrs. Park told Cindy when she dismounted. Undoubtedly she was pleased.

Cindy thanked her shyly, filled with gratitude. Now, if ever, she thought, was the time to ask if she might be assigned to Banner. Caring for him, day after day, week in and week out, would make him almost as much *her* horse as Laurel Proctor's. She was allowed to lead him back to the stable and help rub him down, but not until the last minute did she find courage to broach the question.

Then she approached it in a roundabout way. "Please, Mrs. Park, can you tell me when you'll make the assignments?"

"I'm not sure yet. Perhaps by the end of the week." She smiled at Cindy across Banner's back. "There's no great hurry."

Cindy's pounding heart seemed to leap to her throat. How could she bear to wait that long? Did she dare ask to have Banner as her special charge, or was Caro right: Would this be considered too aggressive? Her better judgment prevailed, and she said nothing, but as she bicycled off toward Oak Bluffs, she regretted that she had been so hesitant. And now the opportunity was gone!

Once again the clouds met overhead to block out the late-afternoon sun. The sky grew so dark that Cindy started to pedal faster, fearing a long, wet ride home. A few fat drops were falling as she entered the steamship office, where, in spite of the five minutes left until closing time, there was a waiting line.

She took her place as the rain began to pelt the rooftop of the one-story building. Turning toward the door to regard the cloudburst dismally, she watched a tall, long-necked boy with hair so fair it was almost white come racing inside, then stand and shake himself like a soaked puppy.

"Wow," he said, and grinned at Cindy, who was trying to find the cord that adjusted the hood of her yellow slicker.

With the natural good manners of an islander greeting a summer stranger, Cindy smiled in return, although this wasn't summer and the boy looked exceptionally out of place. He was wearing a navy blue jacket with a school insignia on the pocket, an open-throat striped shirt, and loafers. To Cindy, accustomed to the jeans and casual sweaters or T-shirts of her classmates, he looked dressed up. How had he happened to seek shelter here on this stormy afternoon? she wondered. A ferry from Woods Hole had docked just before she arrived at the terminal, but the passengers had scattered hastily to cars and taxis, anticipating the storm.

She edged forward in the slow-moving line, which the boy made no attempt to join. Instead, he stood at a window, peering out at the rain through the clouded glass as if he were looking for someone.

When Cindy had finished her exchange with the office clerk, the stranger was still there.

Cindy herself was brought up short in the doorway. As a man in line ahead of her made a dash for his parked car, the boy at the window turned toward her and raised his hands to make quotation marks with his fingers. "Have a nice day!"

"Tomorrow," Cindy replied, watching the rain pound down on her bicycle, which was parked in an empty rack outside the building.

In the manner of a stranded traveler the boy continued the conversation. "You live here?"

"In Oak Bluffs, no. On the island, yes," replied Cindy, thinking of the long ride home.

"And you're in high school?"

"How did you guess?" She glanced at the emblem on the stranger's jacket again but refrained from saying there were no private schools on Martha's Vineyard.

"I'm new," the boy told her, as if she couldn't tell. "My name's Kevin Wainwright, like Dad's, but I've always been called Tad."

"Hello, Tad," said Cindy.

"We've just moved here. I haven't even seen the house we're going to live in. It's in a place called Chilmark, if you know where that is."

Cindy burst out laughing. "This island is only eighteen miles long," she told him.

"Is it far from where you live?"

"Far enough." Cindy turned cautious. "Chilmark's up-island."

Tad didn't question the expression, although it must have sounded odd to his nonnative ears. "I'm starting school late," he said, "if they'll let me."

"They'll let you," predicted Cindy.

"It's going to be sort of strange, not knowing anybody," Tad continued, running his fingers through his pale hair. Then, quite suddenly, he smiled in a manner that transformed his face. In spite of his beaky nose and unremarkable hazel eyes, Cindy thought he looked endearingly boyish.

"You'll meet people quickly," she promised, trying to sound comforting and conceal her impatience for the rain to let up so that she could be on her way.

"Hey, maybe we'll be in the same class!"

"I'm a sophomore," said Cindy, noticing that the clerk, who had been shuffling papers on the counter during the heavy shower, was making motions toward closing up.

"I'll be a junior," said Tad. "Say, could I have your phone number in case I need to ask any questions about school?"

Cindy realized that the boy was looking at her with shy admiration, although she couldn't imagine why. In her threadbare jeans and plaid woolen shirt she felt like a disheveled sparrow standing next to a white-crested crane.

"My—my phone number?" she stammered.

"Sure. Why not?" Tad pulled a pen from his pocket and was fumbling for a piece of paper in his wallet, but apparently the only thing he could find was a five-dollar bill. He pulled it out and tested the pen on the margin, then stood waiting.

Why not indeed? This boy only wanted to ask a few questions. Besides, it might be fun to get to know him better. Hastily Cindy dictated the number, then watched the clerk, keys in hand, saunter toward the door.

"Rain or no rain," he said, "you kids'll have to get out of here."

As if on cue a bright red Ford pickup truck came touring along the street, raising a wake of water from the macadam. "Dad!" cried the boy, and was through the door in a second while Cindy watched the truck skidding to a halt.

"Sorry about this, girlie," said the clerk as he held the door ajar.

"Never mind. I won't melt." Cindy hurried toward the bicycle rack, head down against the rain, only to meet Tad head-on.

"Get in the cab," he commanded as he snatched the bike from the rack and heaved it into the back of the truck.

"But you don't even know where I live! Your father—"

Ignoring such a weak protest, Tad hurried Cindy up the high step and into the broad seat next to an older man who had Tad's same pale hair and lean frame. "Wainwright Rescue Squad," he said as Tad got in and slammed the door. "You lead the way, young lady."

"Take County Road to the Edgartown Road," Cindy told him. "You can drop me off there, and thank you!"

"My pleasure," said Mr. Wainwright. "Just tell me where to turn." He inspected Cindy quickly, his eyes twinkling. "You look like a wet canary," he added, then leaned forward over the steering wheel to peer at the headlights approaching cautiously through the rain. "Tad hasn't told me your name."

"Because I don't know it," Tad admitted with a laugh.

"You mean this pretty girl's a pickup, son? You have good taste."

Although she knew she was being teased, Cindy was embarrassed and slightly indignant. "I'd rather be called an orphan of the storm than a pickup," she told Tad's father.

"Spoken like a true islander," replied the man, chuckling. He turned and looked at her again. "You still haven't told us your name."

"Cynthia Foster," said Cindy, wriggling uncomfortably. She felt crushed in the small cab and stifled by the closed dampness.

"Let's get some air in here," suggested Tad, and rolled down his window.

Cindy breathed in relief and occupied herself with giving the necessary directions. Once County Road was reached and Mr. Wainwright had headed inland, the storm petered out and the roads became almost dry. Conversation petered out, too, when Mr. Wainwright switched the car radio dial to the news.

At the turn into the Edgartown Road Cindy said, "If you'll pull to the right and drop me off here, I'll be just fine."

"Sure we can't take you right to the door?"

"No, thank you, really!"

Cindy waved as the pickup sped away and called, "Thank you again," then mounted her bike and headed for Caroline's house, as she had promised.

CHAPTER
3

ABSORBED BY HER OWN CONCERNS, Caroline scarcely noticed that Cindy's clothes were wet and that she dropped her slicker thoughtfully in the entryway. "Come on up to my room," she said at once. "I'm having a terrible time deciding."

"Deciding?" asked Cindy, half forgetting the purpose of her visit.

"What to wear, silly. On Saturday night."

"Oh, yes." Cindy supposed she should be flattered that Caroline wanted to consult her, but instead, she was wondering what could be so important about a date with Johnny Trumbull, whom she had undertaken to beat up in third grade.

At recess one morning Johnny had been teasing a harmless garter snake with a stick, and when Cindy heard him threatening to kill it, she stepped between the pudgy boy and his victim, doubled her fist, and punched Johnny in the stomach. Yelping, Johnny whacked her across the shins with his stick. Cindy still remembered how much it had hurt! Suddenly they were rolling on the ground in a furious fight that brought a teacher on the run. Hauled to her feet, Cindy rubbed her shins and refused to cry.

And here Caroline was in a swivet about how best to impress this same Trumbull boy, now a big, brawny youth with a football player's carriage. As Caroline tried on three dresses in turn, Cindy sank down on the floor, leaned against the foot of the bed, and wondered what Caroline and Johnny would find to talk about.

Football, she supposed. Certainly not horses. She doubted that Caroline, who seemed bent on creating a feminine image, would even mention that she had joined the 4-H program.

"Well, what do you think, Cindy?"

"You look great in all of them, Caro," Cindy said sincerely. Caroline's blue eyes and flyaway hair were far better suited to dresses than to jeans.

"But *which*?"

"Wear the blue," said Cindy decisively. "I've really got to get home."

Not a word had Cindy said about her introductory ride on the black pony or about her encounter in Oak Bluffs, yet in bed that night she thought a lot about both incidents. She lay hoping and finally persuading herself that Banner would indeed be given into her charge and anticipated the months to come with tremulous excitement. When her thoughts shifted to the Wainwrights, it was the father who first claimed her attention. Mr. Wainwright's conversation had baffled her. He had said "this pretty girl," which no one had ever done before. Because Cindy thought of herself—if she thought at all—as plain, she wondered if Tad's father had been joking. She also wondered what work he planned to do on the island. Although he was driving a truck, his well-cared-for hands weren't those of a laborer, and Tad was obviously a product of private school.

Was that why he seemed so different from the Vineyard boys? Or was it the way in which he had approached her, easily yet somewhat tentatively, as though he were testing his own responses to an island girl. Although Tad wasn't conventionally good-looking his white-blond hair was so conspicuous that it gave him a certain style. Besides, he had an off-island air about him that she found attractive. In fact, she rather wished he were going to be in her classes. A new face would be as welcome as a breath of fresh air.

Drowsily Cindy wondered if he would phone her as he had suggested or whether he had forgotten the telephone number written on the five-dollar bill. He might even have spent it, for all she knew. Yawning, she turned over, punched up her pillow, and fell asleep.

Cindy awakened to a mild and sunny morning. Friday was always a day when impatience gripped her along with her classmates. Everyone was anxious to get the school week over with, to break loose.

The hours dragged, but the afternoon was still cloudless when Cindy and Caroline reached Heathorfield Farm. They went at once to the barn, where they found Mrs. Park instructing the Bowman twins and two new recruits on their duties for the coming week. There was still no list of assignments.

Nevertheless, for Cindy the weekend was a happy one. She went back to the farm on Saturday morning and had a chance to work with Mrs. Park, who was attempting to gentle the palomino. "Easy, girl, easy, Flax," she kept saying in a soothing voice as she taught the lessons necessary before the mare could be trusted with novice riders.

"It usually takes more than a year to teach a horse to work safely with the handicapped," she told Cindy. "Banner is a shoo-in, and I've got four other horses I can count on, but I really need a sixth."

After half an hour she dismounted and put Cindy up on Flax. "Let her canter around the field for a bit; then bring her back here and see if you can teach her to act like a lady."

The mare was a handful. When she found a stranger in the saddle, she reared, then hit the ground with her front hooves and danced backward. Cindy tried to hide her alarm and hung on, but her heart was racing and her knees grew weak. Then, determined to take command, she forced her legs to grip Flax's sides. Nudging the mare with her left heel, she got her started on a proper course close to the encircling fence.

The palomino fairly flew over the grassy pasture, kicking up turf and shaking her head irascibly, but after a couple of turns she gave up the contest of wills and settled into a trot and finally a walk, belatedly obeying Cindy's directions. When she came to a stop before Mrs. Park, Flax's eyes were bulging, as if she were shocked at being forced to obey.

"Good girl!"

Cindy couldn't tell whether this praise was directed to her or to the mare. When she slid from the saddle to the ground, she felt momentarily wobbly, but she had the satisfaction of knowing that she had passed an important test. There would be other tests to come, of course, but for the moment Cindy was content. She felt that Mrs. Park still approved of her, that they would get along.

After church on Sunday Caroline came over to the Fosters' to tell Cindy about her date with Johnny. Peter had gone with his parents to pick late raspberries at a nearby farm, and the two girls sat on the porch steps in the early-afternoon sun.

"Did you have a good time last night?" Cindy asked at once.

Caroline nodded dreamily. "Johnny seems so much older than he did last year. He doesn't horse around as much. And he's really into football, Cindy. If he makes it here on the island, as he's hoping to, he might even have a chance at a college scholarship."

"Wow, that'd be great," Cindy responded. "What movie did you see?"

"An old film from the fifties," Caroline said. "It wasn't much." She giggled reminiscently. "Just an excuse, really, to turn out the lights."

The phone rang, interrupting any further confidences. As Cindy got up to answer, she said, "Come on in. Let's get something cool to drink." She picked up the receiver while Caroline followed. "Hello."

"Cynthia?" asked a masculine voice.

Nobody ever called her Cynthia. "This is Cindy."

There was a chuckle at the other end of the line. "Cindy, then. I was wondering if you had a nickname."

"Who's this?"

"Tad Wainwright. You said I could phone."

"Oh, yes, to ask questions."

"Yeah. Well, it's this way. I'm supposed to show up tomorrow at school, and I need to know—what should I wear?"

If one more person asks me what to wear, I'm going to go bananas, Cindy thought as she controlled an impulse to giggle. "Oh, anything," she said.

"No, seriously?"

"Jeans, any old shirt, running shoes or sneakers. Loafers look too preppy."

"Ha! That was a dig!"

"Sorry," Cindy said apologetically. "I didn't mean to be rude, just—"

"Forget it," Tad interrupted, then asked with a trace of new-boy anxiety, "Is there anything else I ought to know?"

"Nothing I can think of," replied Cindy. "You'll do all right." More than all right, she thought. Tad was a standout, with his white-blond hair, his rangy build, his naturally easy manner. She found herself asking, "Do you play football?" while Caroline stood by, looking puzzled. She held a glass of cranberry juice out to Cindy, who took it with a nod of thanks.

At the other end of the line Tad replied, "No. I row. Or used to."

"Row?"

"Like in a boat. A scull actually." Tad sounded amused.

"Oh." Aware of how unsophisticated he must think her, Cindy searched for a way to end this conversation but hesitated a moment too long.

"Do you play tennis?" Tad asked.

"Not really. I ride."

"Ride?"

It was Cindy's turn to laugh. "Like on horseback," she said. Then she plucked up courage to add, "Look, I've got to go now. I have a guest." She looked across the room at Caroline, who had settled down on the sofa, and made a wry face of apology.

"Who was that?" asked Caroline as soon as the receiver was put down. A good friend was permitted frank curiosity.

"Just a boy I happened to meet down by the ferry dock. He's starting school here."

Caroline's blue eyes probed Cindy's. "Our age?"

"A little older. He'll be a junior."

"Even better. Is he—well, what's he like?"

Cindy shrugged. "How should I know?" Neither she nor Caroline had ever pursued casual contacts with off-island kids. Although this, of course, was different. Tad was going to live here. "I just talked to him for a few minutes," she explained.

"Do you know his name?"

Cindy nodded. "Tad Wainwright. He's tall, skinny. Mom would say he has nice manners. The preppy type."

Caroline's interest increased. "D'you think he'll ask you for a date?"

"Of course not. I told you, he's older."

Yet after Caroline had left for home, Cindy's thoughts returned to the telephone conversation, which she had broken off before finding out whether Tad was interested in horses, whether indeed, he could ride. Then she shook herself loose from a nebulous idea. The new boy was just a chance acquaintance who might not even recognize her if she passed him in the high school hall.

However, that shock of white hair was unmistakable. Cindy would recognize *him*. And she did, a few days later, and asked with a smile, "How are things going. Okay?"

"Peachy-keen," replied Tad, clowning. "I've got a new nickname."

"Whitey," said Cindy. "Word gets around."

"What are you doing after school?" Tad asked unexpectedly.

"Going over to Heatherfield Farm. I'm in a 4-H horse program," Cindy told him.

"How about tomorrow?"

"Same thing."

"Do you have to go *every* day?"

I don't have to go, Cindy could have replied, but I want to. Instead, she said, "For a while. We're working with horses in training to be ridden by handicapped kids." Before she could explain further, the third-period bell rang, and she and Tad hurried on, moving off in opposite directions.

Caroline entered the chemistry classroom behind Cindy. "Is *that* the boy?" she whispered.

Cindy nodded, knowing it was useless to pretend she didn't understand.

"Wow! He's really something."

"He doesn't play football," Cindy told her mischievously.

The teacher slapped some books on his desk and cleared his throat, forestalling further conversation. Cindy liked chemistry and became absorbed, but Caroline doodled on the page of an open notebook. Anything involving mathematics bored her.

Not until that afternoon at the farm did the girls have a chance to talk again, and then it was under strained circumstances. The assignment list had at last been posted, and Cindy discovered, to her acute dismay, that she had been given the care of the palomino while Banner was put in Caroline's charge.

At first glance she could scarcely believe it. Over the past week she had come to think of Banner as *her* pony, hers to curry, hers to call to the pasture fence and feed with purloined apples. When allowed to ride him, she was in seventh heaven, and his pliancy testified to the fact that he returned her devotion.

No! Cindy wanted to scream at the list on the wall. Her disappointment was barely controllable. Yet she recognized that Mrs. Park was not being unfair. She was awarding her the most difficult horse of the lot as a challenge. Caroline could handle Banner well enough, as could any of the other girls. But whether Flax could be tamed sufficiently to work with novice riders was anybody's guess.

Caroline peered over Cindy's shoulder at the list. "I get Banner? I guess I'm lucky."

"I'll say!" Cindy surprised herself by getting her voice under control. She turned away quickly and walked over to the palomino's stall.

"You really wanted the black pony, didn't you?" asked Caroline, following.

"Don't rub it in," Cindy muttered.

"I'd offer to trade, but I'm scared to death of Flax," Caroline admitted.

"Oh, she's not so bad once she knows who's boss," Cindy said, although she knew in her heart that mastering the mare brought no satisfaction. She wanted to make friends with the horse, not subdue her.

Making friends, however, didn't seem to appeal to Flax at all. She bridled and bucked, rolled her eyes wickedly, and tried to nip Cindy's arm if given half a chance. By the end of the afternoon Cindy was thoroughly disheartened.

Only Helen Park seemed optimistic. "You're making some headway," she said cheerfully as Cindy rubbed Flax down, then added more quietly, "There's not a girl in the group who could handle her the way you do."

As she led Banner into the next stall, Caroline overheard. "She needs a strong boy on her back, that's what she needs," she said to Mrs. Park. "Aren't we going to get any boys in this program?"

"I doubt it, Caroline. All over the country the story's the same. Taking care of horses just doesn't appeal to boys your age."

Caroline accepted this with a regretful sigh. "I guess they're more interested in sports."

By mid-October the football season was well under way. The Vineyard team had played several rival teams in the Mayflower League, made up of schools from small towns on the Massachusetts mainland, but it was the Thanksgiving game with the Nantucket Whalers that everyone anticipated. The Harvard-Yale game in Cambridge wasn't nearly as important to islanders as the offshore game that would take place on a windswept field thirty miles south of Cape Cod.

This year it would be an away game, and the high school players were anticipating a crowd of perhaps a thousand when they met their foes across the Muskeget Channel. Caroline was caught up in the seasonal feeling of excitement and was hoping to be chosen as one of the cheerleaders who would make the trip. Cindy, on the other hand, only feigned enthusiasm. Her heart and mind were wholly concerned with horses.

And with Banner in particular. She told her mother, sorrowfully, that she had been put in charge of the unruly palomino instead of the pony she had hoped for. But she was cheered when Mrs. Park told her she could ride Banner on Saturday mornings if she wanted to spend extra time at the farm.

"If you finish your chores here first," Mrs. Foster agreed with a nod.

The chores weren't too onerous. On Saturday morning it took Cindy less than an hour to scrub the bathroom and mop the kitchen floor. Peter, meanwhile, dawdled over his tasks of emptying trash and sweeping out the garage, which at this time of year abounded with dead leaves. When Cindy went out to get her bike, she found her brother in the driveway playing with the kitten—teasing him, actually—with a small boy's indifference to the irritation of his pet.

Silver had only one thought, to get away from his persecutor, but every time he tried to break loose, Peter pulled him back by his tail.

"Don't do that!" Cindy scolded. "You're hurting him!"

"Aw, he doesn't mind. We're just having fun." Peter was not about to be reprimanded by his older sister.

"*You're* having fun, maybe. Not Silver!" Cindy snatched the kitten from the ground and cradled it in her arms, but the little animal was by now so distraught that he turned and hissed at her.

Peter, in turn, was furious. Springing to his feet, he cried, "Hey, he's mine, not yours."

He made a grab for the cat, but Cindy slapped his arm with her free hand. "I'm taking him into the house to Mom right now." She marched off toward the kitchen steps while Peter followed, holding his arm and screaming "Waah!" in simulated pain.

Mrs. Foster, having seen the episode from the kitchen window, was quite prepared when her children confronted her. "She hit me, Mom," wailed Peter, while Cindy, still stroking the frightened kitten, said, "He's got to learn not to hurt animals!"

"Peter, I'm ashamed of you," said Mrs. Foster. "One more such incident, and Silver will be given away." Then she turned to her daughter. "You must never strike your brother, or anyone else, in anger. Cindy, I'm ashamed of you, too."

CHAPTER
4

PENITENTLY CINDY PEDALED off toward the farm. She was unaccustomed to being reproved by her mother. Usually they acted more like sisters who enjoyed each other's company than like parent and child. Yet she felt a lingering indignation over Peter's treatment of the kitten. In that long-ago episode with Johnny Trumbull and the garter snake she remembered having the same reaction, and when she saw a rider use a whip on a horse she actually flinched.

The morning was windless with a few thin scraps of fog still clinging to the water in the lagoon. The farm road was dry and dusty, and the fields had a purplish cast that would remain until the first snowfall. Gradually Cindy was soothed by the peacefulness of the scene. She loved the island in the fall and winter, when it belonged to the people who lived here year-round.

The quiet was suddenly torn, however, by a gaggle of African geese, led by a hissing gander, that came scuttling across the farm lane in the path of her bicycle. Their wings outspread in wild alarm, they looked at Cindy in fury, but the moment she braked to a halt, they slowed to a solemn strut.

In the stable Caroline was mucking out Banner's stall. "How come you didn't do it yesterday?" Cindy asked.

"I didn't have time." Caroline looked disheveled, bored, and faintly nauseated. "This isn't girls' work," she said plaintively.

"Whatever happened to women's lib?" Cindy teased, then quickly relented. "Here! I'll help you." Together they made short work of forking out the old shavings, disinfecting the floor, and putting down fresh bedding. "Where's Banner?" Cindy paused to ask.

"In the lower pasture. Mrs. Park had to give him a shot. He's got asthma."

"Asthma? You mean he's having trouble breathing?"

"Don't worry. She says it's not serious."

Nevertheless, Cindy hurried down to the field, where Banner was standing patiently by the gate, looking up toward the house and wheezing at intervals. Close by, Helen Park was mending a break in the fence.

"Hi, Cindy," she called, then sat back on her heels. "If you're going riding, take one of the other horses instead of Banner. His asthma's kicking up, and he needs a rest."

"Poor boy," murmured Cindy as she reached out to stroke the pony's neck. In a worried voice she said, "You're sure it's nothing serious?"

Mrs. Park shook her head. "It comes and goes. We let him stay outside overnight when the weather's mild. Fresh air seems to help."

Relieved, Cindy decided she would take Flax for a canter through the woods, then bring her back and work with her in the ring for a while, hoping that after some strenuous exercise she would be more amenable.

On returning from a two-mile workout, however, Flax was as ornery as ever, prancing and bucking in a determined effort to shake Cindy off her back. Mrs. Park wasn't in sight, but a young man was standing on the brow of the hill, looking down on the exercise ring from a vantage point near the barn. Wearing a wide-brimmed hat and a lumber jacket he looked, from Cindy's distance, like a picture of an Australian bushman. Then, as he sauntered down the hill and came closer, she got a better look. Reining Flax in firmly, she called in surprise, "Tad! What are you doing here?"

"Admiring your horsemanship." Tad pushed his hat to the back of his head and asked, "Do you give lessons?"

Ignoring the question, Cindy asked in turn, "How did you find me?"

"I phoned your house. Your mother told me where to look. So I tried the stable and a very nice girl groom gave me further directions. Mission completed."

Cindy burst out laughing. "Caroline's not a girl groom. She's a member of the 4-H horse program, just like me."

"I'll apologize if I see her again," Tad promised.

"Oh, you'll see her. Caroline likes boys," Cindy said as Flax impatiently pawed the ground.

"And you don't?"

Cindy flushed, aware that she had sounded sarcastic rather than friendly. Instead of replying to Tad's teasing, she returned her attention to the palomino, letting her dance around for a few minutes, then bringing her to a halt and dismounting. "Want to hold her reins while I take off the saddle?" she suggested. "Flax, hold still like a good girl."

Cindy let the mare loose in an empty pasture, then walked up the hill with Tad, who carried the saddle to the barn. She led him into the tack room, told him where to put it, then took him on a tour of the stable and introduced him to the few horses still in their stalls. Caroline had disappeared.

Tad was politely interested, but he didn't linger at any one stall or even reach out to touch a horse. "I was thinking," he said when they came back into the sunlight, "that you might like to drive out and take a look at the house. Your mother said it would be all right if you had time."

Good for Mom, giving me an out, thought Cindy, although she felt quite willing to go with this casually friendly boy. "I'd like to see your house," she said, "but I have my bike."

"No problem. The bike has been in the back of tho pickup before."

So Cindy found herself riding up-island along a familiar road that led through the dense shade of thick pine woods alternating with open farmland, sloping meadows, and scattered ponds. "Now that you've been here a couple of weeks," she said, "how do you like the Vineyard?"

"It's pretty nice. Beautiful, in fact. But there's not much to do, is there?"

"Enough." Thinking of her early mornings and busy days Cindy added, "I guess island people get used to making their own fun."

"That figures. Like you and your horses."

"They aren't my horses. Some of them belong to Mrs. Park, and others are boarders." As Tad drove along the narrow road with proper caution, Cindy told him how much she was enjoying work at the farm, although she didn't mention how devoted she was to Banner. Nevertheless, by the time he turned in at an open gate, she was quite relaxed, and the animation in her voice indicated that she was enjoying the excursion.

"Here we are." Tad pulled up before the door of a rambling gray farmhouse hugging a rise of ground above a duck pond. Cindy opened the door on her side of the cab and slid to the ground, looking down at her boots and wondering if they were clean enough to wear inside.

"Shall I take them off?"

Tad shook his head. "We're still getting settled."

There was no center hall to the house. The room they entered was small, with a low-beamed ceiling and a fireplace stretching almost the width of one wall. As the daughter of a master carpenter Cindy looked around admiringly. This place had been carefully restored.

"Hey, Dad!"

A voice called, "Back here!" and Cindy was led to a sunny room lined, floor to ceiling, with bookcases. Most of them were empty, although there were dozens of unpacked cartons cluttering the floor.

Mr. Wainwright, wearing an out-at-the-elbows gray sweater, stepped over a stack of books to greet Cindy without indicating that her arrival was unexpected. "Welcome to my workroom," he said with a rueful smile, "and I mean *work*room." Having seen him only in the cab of the truck, Cindy was surprised by his height. He was even taller than Tad, and like Tad, he had a charismatic quality.

"Wow!" Cindy breathed in amazement as her glance roved around the room. "Somebody here must read a lot."

"My father's a writer," explained Tad with pride.

Cindy had never met a writer. "You mean, that's your business?" she asked Mr. Wainwright curiously.

"You might say so. It's what I do for a living."

"Or did," put in Tad. "Looks as if you'll spend a couple of years just getting this room settled."

Mr. Wainwright looked as though he were tempted to agree. "If only we could get the books sorted into categories—"

"We? No *way*!" said Tad promptly. "Come on, Cindy, I'll show you the rest of the house."

"Wait a minute." Cindy drew back. "Could we help, Mr. Wainwright? I think it might be fun."

Who was more surprised at the offer it was hard to say. "Are you kidding?" Tad asked, although Mr.

Wainwright had the hopeful look of a man seeing light at the end of a tunnel.

"Great! Give me an hour's work, and I'll buy you kids some lunch. How about it?"

Tad's father began making cardboard signs reading HISTORY, FICTION, REFERENCE, TRAVEL, BIOGRAPHY, which he propped on various shelves of the surrounding bookcases, while Tad, grumbling half-heartedly, started opening cartons.

The books were heavier to handle than Cindy expected, but she trotted from shelf to shelf with those she could readily decide how to place. There were some that fitted no category, so new ones had to be added: ART, ESSAYS, HUMOR. After a time the three became a team, Tad opening the cartons and handing stacks of books to Cindy, who carried them to the proper stations, and Mr. Wainwright moving from place to place, arranging them as he saw fit on the shelves.

The longer Cindy worked, the more she was impressed by the scope of a writer's library. "What *kind* of books do you write?" she was prompted to ask after a while.

"Fiction. Historical fiction mostly, but sometimes spy novels for a change of pace."

Another question occurred to her. Where was Tad's mother? There had been no indication of the presence of a woman in the house. Sensibly, however, she didn't voice such a personal query. The answer could wait.

As cartons were emptied, Tad put them on the floor and stamped them flat, then stacked them in a corner ready to be put out with the trash. Gradually the center of the floor was cleared, and when Mr. Wainwright finally suggested, "Time we broke off," Cindy realized that she should call her mother and tell her why she wouldn't be home for lunch.

Mrs. Foster wasn't a fussy mother or an anxious one. She trusted Cindy's judgment and said, "See you later then. Have fun."

"Oh, it *is* fun, Mom. It's like sorting out a public library. You never saw so many books!"

Overhearing, Mr. Wainwright chuckled. "Do you read a lot, Cindy?"

"Not really." She used a sad excuse, which happened to be true in her case, "I never have time." Then she said, "You've got a horse book, though, I'd like to look at."

"Borrow it," suggested Mr. Wainwright when she went to the shelf and plucked it from between its strange companions. He glanced at the title. "Better yet, keep it, but don't give it away. I may want to borrow it back someday."

Tad proposed that instead of their going out for lunch, it would be quicker and easier to cook a frozen pizza and share it in the kitchen. Cindy helped by making a tossed salad with her own French dressing, which the Wainwrights considered far superior to the bottled kind. By midafternoon most of the book boxes were unpacked, and Mr. Wainwright declared himself eternally grateful. "I'll do something for you someday," he promised Cindy, who went off with Tad in the pickup, the horse book protectively carried on her lap.

"You may have wondered about Mom," Tad said unexpectedly when they were about halfway to Vineyard Haven.

"Yes," Cindy admitted.

"She was in publishing, too," Tad told her. "We lived in New York, you see, and she had a real great job as a textbook editor. She died of some crazy galloping kind of cancer six months ago."

"Oh." Cindy couldn't say anything so trivial as "I'm so sorry." She couldn't bring herself to say anything at all for a long minute. Then she asked, "Is that why you moved here?"

Tad nodded. "My father's escaping. He thinks he wants nothing but peace and quiet, but I wonder how long he'll function away from New York."

"A lot of writers live on the Vineyard," said Cindy. "So do theater people and artists. They seem to adjust." She stumbled on, aware that she was out of her depth, that she didn't know what she was talking about since she had never actually met any of them.

"Yeah, but they're mostly retired," said Tad, whose father was probably in his forties and still in mid-career.

Again Cindy felt at a loss, but she managed to say, "There are people who come here and like it at once. There are others who grow into this way of life. Some kids moving from the mainland feel trapped, out of touch with the real world. What about you, Tad?"

"I don't know!" Tad's voice rose and broke momentarily as he pounded a fist on the steering wheel. "I wish I could say I'll get along just fine, but I'm not sure. I didn't mind being hauled out of school because I wanted to be with Pop. He needs me, and a boys' boarding school isn't that great anyway."

"You'll make friends. It takes time." How banal the words sounded, an empty promise.

Tad didn't answer. At Cindy's reminder he turned into Strawberry Hill Road and stopped at the foot of the Fosters' gravel drive, then shifted to park and started to turn the door handle. "Don't get out," Cindy said, with a smile intended to be consoling, but she felt strained and bleak. "Thanks for everything." Impulsively she reached out and, for a split second, covered the hand still on the steering wheel with hers.

CHAPTER

5

UNCHARACTERISTICALLY HELEN PARK seemed apprehensive on the day when the handicapped children were due to arrive for their first experience with riding. "The horses have been behaving nicely for you girls," she told the 4-H group, "but you can't count on them. You can't count on the children either. They may be frightened or headstrong, or they may be very noisy and scare the horses. Their behavior is unpredictable.

"Your role is to be calm and stay that way, especially in an emergency. You'll have lots of help. There will be an adult volunteer on each side of a horse when a child is aboard, and you will be leading, at a slow pace, the horse you have been working with. Later on, when you're sure the horses are tractable, we'll try to teach the children to mount by themselves and hold onto the reins."

"Who's 'we'?" whispered Caroline to Cindy. "Sounds like the grown-ups will be running the show and we'll still be the stable hands."

"Any questions?" Mrs. Park's thick braid of hair swung against her shoulder as she turned toward Caroline.

Caroline shook her head no.

A bus lumbered through the upper gate and came to a halt in a patch of trampled field grass near the barn. Mrs. Park went to meet it, but the girls stayed in a group and watched the children and the 4-H leaders come down the bus steps.

Cindy counted ten children and five instructors. One little boy looked no more than eight years old, but most of the others seemed to be ten or eleven. There were more boys than girls.

At first, except for the youngest child, who started to run around in ever-widening circles, most of the children seemed subdued. Cindy noticed, as they trudged down the lane toward the practice field, that several were carrying helmets used to protect the heads of inexperienced riders in case of a fall.

This first day, Mrs. Park explained, was more of an introduction period than a riding exercise. The children were encouraged to climb on the fence and lean over to pat Banner, who was led back and forth by Caroline. He was as agreeable as usual and seemed to welcome the newcomers.

Cindy and the other girls paraded their mounts out of the reach of the children, and Mrs. Park introduced each of them by name. Flax, looking beautiful but behaving badly, rolled her eyes and swished her tail impatiently. One timid little girl started to cry.

"Don't be frightened," said a volunteer soothingly. "You know the Flying Horses on the carousel in Oak Bluffs? You're not afraid of them, are you?"

"No," wailed the child. "But these are *alive.*"

"Does anybody want to get up on a horse's back?" asked Mrs. Park after a while. There was a lot of negative headshaking, but the eight-year-old who had been running in circles started to jump up and down.

"Me, me, me!"

"All right, Roy, you'll be the first." One of the volunteers came through the gate and lifted the child onto Banner's saddle. Another quickly joined her, and together they managed to shorten the stirrups sufficiently for Roy's short legs to reach them.

Caroline stood waiting at the pony's head.

Cindy didn't see the small parade that followed because Flax had become so restless that she led her away from the other horses and tried to calm her down. Mrs. Park, noticing the problem, called, "Better move her into the next field, Cindy."

By the time she returned, having carefully closed the connecting gate, a fat girl, giggling uncontrollably, had been led over to the mounting block and was being helped up on a docile twelve-year-old gelding named Dominic. She was inappropriately dressed in a very full skirt and wore an artificial flower in her hair. However, she seemed to be having the time of her life until, quite unexpectedly, her expression changed to horror and she shrieked, "Get me out of here! I'm going to be killed!"

Kicking and screaming, she was helped down again and persuaded by one of the adult helpers to walk back toward the farmhouse. As they left, Cindy could hear the woman talking to the child in a kindly fashion as though nothing unusual had happened.

As an enforced bystander Cindy became deeply impressed by the calmness of the women who acted as volunteers. Several were young mothers, one of whom had a mentally retarded child of her own in the group. Others were teachers, fitting this extra activity into their busy schedules.

Although her responsibility lay with the horses rather than with the children, Cindy was stirred by compassion for these girls and boys. She hoped they would become familiar with the good smell of horse-flesh, be led to run their hands over the smooth coats, learn that the big, unfamiliar animals were gentle, and therefore begin to feel safe with them.

Heading for home later in the afternoon she said to Caroline, "Well, what do you think?"

"I think the whole thing's a waste of time." Caroline's frown was disturbed, but her voice was sharp. "Those kids will never really learn to ride."

"Maybe not," Cindy agreed, "but it will give them an experience they'd never have otherwise."

"So what?" Pent-up anger sparked in Caroline's voice. "I can't take it any longer. I'm opting out!"

"You mean, leaving the program?" Cindy was shocked.

"That's exactly what I mean."

"But you love to ride, Caro!"

"Ride, yes! When a horse is saddled and waiting. I do *not* love mucking out stalls. I do *not* love getting dust in my hair from a currycomb. I cannot stand the smell of horse urine. And those kids make me want to burst into tears."

"But maybe we can help," said Cindy. As Caroline braked her bike and rowed to a stop with her booted feet, Cindy backed up to a spot beside her.

"You can't just walk out," she said argumentatively.

"I can and I will! I have better things to do than playing nursemaid to a horse. I'm a cheerleader, remember? And I may even get to go to the Nantucket game!"

"Is one football game all that important?"

"You bet it is!" Caroline retorted. "And if you had a little more school spirit, you'd think so, too."

With that last thrust Caroline raced off, pumping along without stopping to walk her bike as she usually did on a steep grade. Cindy followed slowly, shaken and depressed. She *had* been wrong in persuading Caro to join the program. Perhaps because riding horseback had been a mutual interest for so long a time, she had been looking straight ahead, like a pony with blinders. Caroline had changed while she had become even more committed to the animals she dearly loved.

Not that she felt drawn to each and every horse with whom she came in contact. Flax could be irritating, Dominic was stolid and dull, but a pony like Banner was like a flag flying. He made her feel happy and capable of great things. The fact that Caroline could desert Banner so casually made Cindy feel, for the first time, that their friendship was in jeopardy.

That night, when her homework was finished and

her parents were absorbed by a television documentary, she went up to her room, undressed, and settled against the pillows on her bed with Mr. Wainwright's book. She needed something—anything—to take her mind off Caroline's decision.

The book, as the title indicated, was concerned with the history of horses, from the fossil remains of Dawn Horse, dating back fifty-five million years, through the evolutionary changes that led to the much larger and faster animal of today. Cindy read listlessly at first, then with increasing interest. When her mother knocked on the door and came in to say good night, she was thoroughly absorbed. "Hey, listen to this, Mom. Did you know that when a horse is cropping grass, he can see all around, both ahead and behind, without moving his head or eyes? Wow, that's really something!"

Mrs. Foster sat down on the foot of her daughter's bed. "What are you reading?"

"A book Mr. Wainwright lent me. Well, gave me actually. Do you suppose he's read all the books he has in that house?"

"It's possible but rather unlikely." Mrs. Foster reached out and put a hand around Cindy's ankle, which had escaped from the covers. "You were unusually quiet at dinner," she said. "Is something bothering you?"

"Sort of. Caro's fed up with the horse program.

She's getting out." Cindy slapped the book shut and put it on her night table.

"Well," said her mother after a moment's thought, "that's her decision, not yours. Why are you angry?"

"Because I think she's a rotten sport," muttered Cindy, leaving unsaid the truer words: Because I'll miss her.

"Maybe she has other, more demanding interests," suggested Mrs. Foster.

"Sure. Cheerleading and football and boys, boys, boys!"

"Girls your age veer off in different directions, Cindy. Caroline may be through her horse phase sooner than you."

"With me it isn't a phase. I'll never change!"

"Perhaps not." Mrs. Foster, sounding mildly skeptical, brushed Cindy's forehead with her lips. "Sleep well."

The next day was cold and stormy, but in spite of the weather, there was a last-period pep rally because the all-important Thanksgiving game with Nantucket was little more than a week away. The student body, Cindy among them, sat in bleachers on either side of the gym floor while the cheerleaders, gaily dressed in short uniforms, did everything from cartwheels to pirouettes to boost school spirit to even greater heights.

Caroline, it was easy to see, loved every minute of the drama. When the team members, wearing their numbered game jerseys, leaped out one by one, grinning at the audience and slapping each other's backs, she seemed carried away, bouncing up and down like a rubber ball. Cindy felt sure that she shouted longer and louder than anyone else.

After the entire squad had been assembled on the gym floor, the captain stepped forward like a commanding general and shouted to his men, "What do we eat?"

"Whale meat!"

"What?"

"Whale meat!" The rafters reverberated with the noise, and a girl sitting next to Cindy put her hands over her ears. Then she, too, began to scream at the top of her lungs as the team members formed a circle in the center of the gym and cried, "Fight, fight, FIGHT!" to the delight of more than four hundred students in the bleachers.

Because of the stormy weather, there would be no outdoor practice this afternoon, but as the crowd left the gym for buses and waiting cars, the coach began putting his team members through some light kickoff drills. Caroline was one of three cheerleaders who stayed behind, moving up the bleachers to the fifth row to huddle in conversation. Although Cindy passed within a few feet of her, Caroline didn't notice. She looked happy and so absorbed that Cindy felt a momentary twinge of envy.

A minute later, going through the doors to the main hall, she found herself rubbing elbows with Tad Wainwright. "Hi," he said cheerfully. "You're just the girl I want to see."

Cindy backed off and looked up at him. "Oh?"

"If it clears up over the weekend, how about taking a walk on the beach out at Gay Head?"

Cindy hesitated. "I have to work at the farm tomorrow morning."

"So I'll pick you up there."

Swept onward and away by the crowd surging into the hall behind her, Cindy had to make a quick decision. She loved Gay Head, where dramatic cliffs towered in a rose and gray wall above the sandy shore. Moreover, she welcomed a chance to get to know Tad better. He was interesting, quite different from the boys with whom she had grown up. "All right," she called across a couple of shorter heads. "About eleven?"

Tad grinned, managed to raise his right arm in spite of the pressure of the throng, and made an *O* with his thumb and forefinger. Then he went off toward the pickup while Cindy dashed through the rain to the waiting bus.

She wore her muck boots to the farm the next morning, but she took sneakers along in her bicycle basket. The sky was still cloud-tossed but the storm had blown out over the Atlantic, and the breeze was light and refreshing. When she arrived, Mrs. Park was working with Flax in the exercise ring outside the barn. As soon as she had cleaned the palomino's stall, Cindy went out and called, "Want me to take over?"

Mrs. Park shook her head, then rode over to the doorway in which Cindy was standing. Flax was being skittish and even for such a seasoned rider was hard to handle, but finally she came to a halt, and Mrs. Park kicked loose from the stirrups and slid to the ground.

"The mare's coming along, thanks to you," she said to Cindy, "but she's out of the handicapped program. I guess no horse under ten years old is really trustworthy."

Cindy took Flax's reins from Mrs. Park's hands. "I'm sorry," she crooned softly to the pretty creature, and stroked her damp neck. "Come along with me. I'll give you a good rubdown."

"I suppose you know that we have another dropout."

"Caroline?"

"She phoned last night. I can't blame her actually. This is a grueling program if you're not really committed."

Cindy gave a nod of assent.

"Horse people are different. You can always spot 'em. You're one of us." She smiled at Cindy in a grudging manner that indicated she was paying her a rare compliment. Then, before turning away, she said, "So now you'll be working with Banner, of course."

Of course! Cindy's mind had not raced to the obvious conclusion, but suddenly elation made her feel as if she were walking on air. When Tad arrived in the pickup, her eyes sparkled joyously. "Guess what?" she cried at once. "I've got Banner back."

"Banner? Who's Banner?"

Belatedly Cindy realized she had never mentioned Banner to Tad, let alone introduced him. She had kept the pony a secret too special to be revealed to a virtual stranger, but now Tad was no longer a stranger. He might even become a friend.

"He's a black pony, a perfect love, the best horse here." Words were inadequate when Cindy tried to describe him. She turned toward Tad as he drove the winding road to Gay Head and attempted to explain what Banner meant to her. "He's very gentle, very *intelligent*. When I go to the fence and ask, 'Do you like me?' he even nods his head!"

"Come on now, Cindy!"

"Well, it looks that way to me. Maybe he knows I've got a carrot in my pocket."

"And he knows which pocket?"

Cindy didn't mind being teased. "Wait till you see him!" Her exuberance lasted for the entire drive. Not until they reached the crest of a hill from which they could see the Gay Head lighthouse and Vineyard Sound in the distance did she stop talking about Banner, then only to say, "I'll tell you where to turn right."

"But aren't the cliffs straight ahead?"

"There's no way down from the bluff," Cindy explained. "We usually take the Lobsterville Road to the beach."

"Who lives around here?" asked Tad as he followed her directions. "It looks awfully empty." The land rolled away in low hills and brown meadows, with only a few clapboard houses in sight.

"Descendants of the original Indians, summer people, a few islanders."

"Ah, Indians!" Tad affected a small boy's breathy voice, then became serious. "Imagine more than three thousand Indians settled here, in wigwams. Boy, they must have had rough winters."

"Some of their descendants go to our school," Cindy told him, "but they're no longer pure-blooded."

"And they no longer live in wigwams," said Tad, "just in dumb little houses like everybody else." At Cindy's suggestion, he pulled off the macadam and parked in the sand facing an eroded dune. "Sure you're going to be warm enough?"

"I hope so, Daddy," said Cindy sweetly, taking her turn at teasing. Before getting out of the cab, she pulled off her boots and put on the raggedy sneakers she had brought along.

Yesterday's storm had washed the sand clean. Seaweed trimmed the high-tide line like black rickrack, but there wasn't a human footprint to be seen. "I hope you like to walk," Cindy said, "because it's quite a trek from here to the cliffs and back."

"Any chance of picking up an Indian arrowhead on the way?"

"You never know. Dad has quite a collection, along with a stone pestle for grinding herbs and a couple of the stone sinkers they used for fishing." Cindy added hopefully, "Beachcombing is always better after a storm."

Striding with a long, easy step on the hard sand near the water, Tad set the pace. With the breeze at their backs it was easy to speak without raising their voices, but for the first mile or so neither one made an effort at conversation. Cindy's head bent toward the scallops of foam left by retreating waves or raised to the gulls wheeling overhead. She was proud to be able to show Tad her island and hoped that he found it beautiful, but this wasn't something she was tempted to talk about.

"Once upon a time," said Tad after a while, assuming the air of an adult telling a story to a child, "there was a great Indian chief called Moped."

"Moshop." Cindy corrected him with a laugh. "He was big, but he wasn't noisy."

"Let me tell the story my way," Tad insisted. "Moped was a giant of a man. He had feet as big as small islands, and he could walk from Cape Cod, where he lived, all the way to the Vineyard in a single afternoon."

"On the water?" asked Cindy.

"*In* the water, dear. He had never met Martha or tasted her grapes, so when he decided to stay here, he called this place Capawack.

"Now this giant had a wife, whose name was Squant. She was almost as big as he was and strong enough to tear up trees by the roots for her cooking fire. That's why there are so few trees on Gay Head." Tad paused for a moment and looked up at a big white gull swooping and screaming at them. "Squant, squant, squant!" he screamed back.

Cindy laughed. Her eyes were bright with mischief, and the sea air had turned her loose curls to ringlets. "Now I'm supposed to ask what the wife cooked," she said. "Do you know the answer?"

"Of course I do. Trust Professor Wainwright. Being a giant, Moped just waded out into the sound, caught a whale by the tail, and killed it by dashing it against the cliff. Say, where are the red cliffs anyway? I don't even see them!"

"You will," promised Cindy. "They're around the corner."

"Do you want to hear the end?" Without waiting for an answer, Tad said, "The whale's blood ran down the cliff in a crimson flood and stained the seawater red. Is it true that the red clay still colors the surf, Cindy?"

"Sometimes, when the tides are high, but not very often. The cliffs are badly eroded."

"So much for civilization," muttered Tad.

"How do you know so much about our Indian legends?" asked Cindy curiously. The combination of myth and nonsense had intrigued her.

"My dear girl, I can read, and we have a few books!"

"Do you read a lot?"

"Sure. Don't you?"

Cindy shook her head. "I never have time."

"A poor excuse, my father would say. We all do what we most want to."

He's right, Cindy thought. I want to take care of horses.

Again they walked along in companionable silence until the beach curved to the left, and there, in clear view, were the sheer clay cliffs topped by the lighthouse.

Those nearest were patterned in gray and beige,

but farther on hints of their former rich colors appeared, and striations of terra-cotta, tan, gray, black, and even whitish clay lay in long ridges on the face of the steep wall. Where the clay met the sand, the colors blended like those on a messy artist's palette, but horizontal streamers up near the summit retained much of their original brilliance.

Tad was impressed. "Hey, that's really great!" He stood and stared upward for several minutes, as though he were trying to memorize the scene.

Cindy bent over a tide pool and picked up a wet lump of clay, icy cold to her touch but becoming malleable as it warmed in her hands. "When I was a little kid, I used to make clay sculptures whenever we picnicked here."

"Don't you still come on picnics? It looks like a perfect spot." Great rocks found nowhere else on the island made the beach below the cliff seem exotic and especially hospitable.

"Not often," said Cindy. "It's crowded in summer. Besides, Dad's too busy with overtime jobs and Mom spends most Saturdays catching up on housework."

Tad turned away from the rocks and stared out over the sound toward the Elizabeth Islands, looming in the distance. He looked sad and preoccupied as they started on the long walk back, then twitched his shoulders as if he were shaking off a weight. Cindy could guess what was wrong. As soon as she had mentioned her mom, he had started thinking about his own mother.

As she would have coaxed an anxious horse into a happier mood, Cindy tried to coax Tad. Horses responded to friendly attention, and so, perhaps, did boys. Knowing that he didn't play football, she nevertheless asked, "Are you going to the Nantucket game?"

"Maybe," he astonished her by saying. "Dad knows this guy in West Tisbury who flies his own Cessna. He's a real football buff, and he's invited Pop and me to go over with him in his plane."

"Does your father like high school football?" asked Cindy in surprise.

"Not especially, but he's keen on local color, and he never knows when he might use a scene like that in a book."

Cindy was really amused. "That's the funniest reason for going to a football game I ever heard of!"

Tad didn't seem to think it as amusing as she did, but to Cindy's relief his mood changed. As they came within sight of the red pickup, he said, "I've got a couple of hoagies and a thermos of coffee in the car. Want to see who can get there first?"

Not because it was expected of her, but because Tad's legs were longer and faster, Cindy lost. She was still gasping when Tad handed her a mug of hot coffee and the delicatessen sandwich. "Mm, good. You certainly manage to think ahead."

CHAPTER

6

"MIND IF I STOP BY OUR HOUSE for a minute?" Tad asked as they left the hills of Gay Head behind them. "It's right on the way."

"I'll race you to the bathroom," Cindy told him candidly, "and this time I'll win."

Tad burst out laughing. "This has been a good day. I think I'm really getting to know you."

"Because of what I just said?"

"Because you're acting natural. You've been pretty standoffish, you know."

Cindy didn't argue, but she thought about Tad's remark after she had reached her own home. She was aware that the walk on the beach had been a breakthrough. She felt more at ease with Tad than she did with any other boy. Since he seemed to demand nothing of her, she was not required to play any of the games at which Caroline seemed so adept.

Her mother and father were going to a neighbor's house for dinner, so Cindy cooked supper for Peter, then sat with him and watched his favorite television show.

"Pretty good, huh?"

"Passable." Cindy had her mind on other things.

At that moment the phone rang, and Tad's voice said, "Cindy, guess what? Pop's friend with the Cessna says it seats four. I can bring along a friend. How about it?"

Surprise made Cindy's reactions slow. Was Tad asking her for a date— a real date rather than a casual encounter? No, two grown-ups would be along. This would be more like a family outing. Then she tried to imagine going up in a Cessna, one of the many small planes that skimmed by daily on a flight line over the back field. It sounded exciting but scary. "I don't know," she said finally.

"What do you mean, you don't know?"

"I've never been up in an airplane," Cindy confessed, but she was ashamed to admit she was frightened.

"You don't have to be worried. Pop says this guy is a very reliable pilot. He used to fly a commercial jet."

"I'll ask my parents," Cindy said. "Can I call you back tomorrow?"

"Do that." Tad sounded slightly disgruntled, as if he had expected her to leap at the invitation.

When she put the receiver back in the cradle, Cindy's brother stared at her with round eyes. "You got a chance to go up in a plane and you didn't grab it?"

"I've got to ask Mom and Dad. You know that."

"But you didn't sound exactly thrilled. You're a dope!"

"It isn't as if it's a big deal, Peter. Just a short flight over to Nantucket for the Thanksgiving game." Cindy tried to hide her fear of flying by assuming an air of superiority.

"The GAME?" Peter spoke the word in capital letters. "You're a double dope! Even the kids in my class are talking about it." He looked at his sister in frank disgust. "Boy, when I'm your age will I sure act different!"

Peter was hanging around enviously when Cindy told her parents about the invitation the next morning. "Who is this Wainwright fellow?" asked Mr. Foster, sounding dubious.

"He's a new boy in school, Dad. A junior. I've

only known him for a few weeks, but I've met his father. He's nice."

"Nice isn't necessarily reliable."

"Mr. Wainwright isn't flying the plane, Dad. It belongs to a former professional pilot."

"Former? An old guy? How old? I'm not sure I want you up in a plane with only one pilot. He might have a heart attack."

"I'm wondering," suggested Cindy's mother, "if we could postpone a firm decision until we have a few more facts. Personally I'd like to meet Tad and talk things over a little more. Cindy, why not ask him to stop by this afternoon?"

"This *afternoon?*" Cindy had been looking forward to going for a ride on Banner. "Oh, Mom, I can't!"

"Why not, dear?"

"I just can't!"

Peter, curled up in a chair, fondling Silver, who was rapidly turning from a kitten into a skinny young cat, looked up and asked, "What gives, Cindy? Are you ashamed of this guy or something?"

"Will you please shut up? This isn't your affair!" Cindy turned to her mother. "All right, I'll ask him, but it won't do any good."

As it happened, however, Tad's visit made all the difference between no and yes. The Fosters found him polite and at ease. He made friends with Peter and calmed Mr. Foster's primary objection to the Nantucket flight by assuring him that his father also had a pilot's license for small planes. By the time he left, Cindy was committed. Although she tried to act nonchalant, she felt ripples of excitement as she thought about the coming trip.

The whole school, for the five days that followed, was in a fever of anticipation. This was the big game of the year, the high point of the season. After the Saturday game and the Thanksgiving holiday it would be downhill all the way to Christmas.

Caroline, sliding into a seat beside Cindy's in study hall, was beaming on Tuesday morning. "I'm one of the four cheerleaders picked to go. Isn't that marvelous?"

"Terrific!" Cindy agreed, aware of how much it meant to her.

"We're even getting new uniforms and new pompoms! The skirts are pleated and very, very short. Wait till you see them!"

Obviously all concern for the horse program had slipped from Caroline's mind. Cindy, however, listened with friendly patience.

"Johnny's still on the squad. Isn't that great? He'll go along with the varsity and may even get to play. Gosh, I wish you could be there, Cindy!"

"I will be," Cindy told her.

Astonishment colored Caroline's eyes a brighter blue. "No kidding? Gee, that's great, really great! We get free flights like the players, but for the fans it costs money." She looked suddenly confused. "Hey, wait a minute. You don't even *like* football."

Cindy burst out laughing until a teacher coming into the room looked at her sharply. Then she ducked her head, opened a book, and whispered to Caroline, "I get a free flight, too. I've been invited to go over in a little Cessna."

"Quiet, please," said the attentive teacher, and that ended the conversation.

Later in the afternoon Cindy went to Heatherfield Farm, where the handicapped children were expected for their second lesson. Banner was still in his stall, so Cindy saddled him quickly and took him for a couple of turns around the practice ring before the bus arrived.

Banner was at his best today, responding to Cindy's horsemanship aids and showing remarkable patience when she subjected him to some of the unpleasant treatment he might expect in the therapy session. She flapped the reins, kicked the pony in the ribs, wiggled around in the saddle, then suddenly went limp and bounced rather than posted to his trot. If Banner showed surprise at these irritations, he didn't show it, and when Cindy got off his back, she expressed her approval by petting him and offering him a carrot as a treat.

"I'm proud of you," Cindy told the pony softly, stroking the black bangs that hung between his expressive eyes. "You're a beauty!" She glanced up the hill. "Here come the children. Remember to stay calm."

Banner seemed to understand. When the bravest of the boys decided to try to mount by himself, he even stretched out his forelegs to lower his back helpfully. Once the child was up, however, his helmet dipped forward suddenly, cutting off his vision, and he lost courage, clutching at Banner's mane.

"Careful, William," said the volunteer at his side soothingly as she reached up and straightened the headgear. "Take the reins now."

The boy obeyed reluctantly, then pulled roughly to balance himself while Cindy watched the pony's reactions. Banner showed no resentment at all. He seemed to accept what was demanded of him, even uncomfortable treatment. She reached up to stroke his neck and murmured sympathy and praise.

It was clear to both the 4-H girls and the volunteers that Banner had quickly become the group's favorite. He was a few hands shorter than the older horses, and he whinnied with a sweet, welcoming sound, not a snort like Dominic's. At the end of the afternoon, after Cindy had returned him to his stall, Mrs. Park said, "You're a rare combination, you and that pony. He trusts you totally."

"I hope so," Cindy replied. "He's very, very special."

Before she left, she told Mrs. Park that she was going to the Nantucket game but would like to come to the farm on Sunday to help with the chores, then go out for a ride through the woods.

"On Banner, of course?"

Cindy smiled. "If possible."

"I'll save him for you," Mrs. Park promised.

When Cindy reached Strawberry Hill Road that afternoon, Caroline was getting off the late bus. Cindy walked her bike the rest of the way and fully expected the coming demand. "I'm dying of curiosity. Tell me everything!"

"There's not all that much to tell. You remember Tad Wainwright, don't you?"

"Of course."

"Well, his father has a friend who flies a small plane. It carries four people. They've asked me to go along."

"They—or he?" Caroline regarded Cindy with increasing interest. "Have you been seeing Tad?"

"Sure. I see him several times a week at school."

"You know perfectly well what I mean!"

"I've never had a date with Tad," said Cindy carefully, "but I've been to his house and met his father, and we've walked on the beach."

"Not dates, just happenings, hmm?"

"You might say so."

"Do you like him?"

"Yes. So would you. He's nice, Caro, and fun in a quiet kind of way. But it isn't a boy-girl thing, not at all."

"Cindy, you're impossible. I suppose Banner is your first and only love?" As Cindy got back on her bike to ride home, she answered her with a noncommittal grin. "Anyway," Caroline called, "I'm glad you're going to see the game. Look me up if you get a chance."

Saturday came too soon. Cindy didn't feel prepared for the trip because of a feeling of apprehension lodged in her stomach like a sodden pancake. She pulled on clean jeans and leg warmers and nervously tugged at the down vest that had been her big present last Christmas. "Won't you need something on your head?" her mother asked.

"I don't think so. It's not *that* cold," Cindy said, but she unearthed an ancient knitted tam-o'-shanter and crammed it into her pocket just in case.

In the fall and winter months there was no direct ferry service between Martha's Vineyard and Nantucket, so everyone going to the game had to travel by plane. Commuter airlines scheduled extra flights, running what amounted to a shuttle service. The tiny waiting room at the airport was packed with people, even though the varsity team, the cheerleaders, and the jayvees had left much earlier.

Cindy's mother dropped her off at the appointed time, but since she couldn't get the car within a hundred yards of the terminal building, all she could say was "Good-bye and have fun, darling," then swing into the exit line. Cindy threaded her way through parents and fans with some consternation. How would she ever find Tad in this crowd?

Suddenly, however, there he was, his platinum hair a beacon above a sea of felt hats and woolen overcoats, tweed caps, and corduroy car jackets. "Tad!" Cindy cried.

"Right here!" He pulled her to his side and carted her off to a gate leading toward a bevy of neatly aligned private planes to the left of the ticket office. "Pop and Jake Resnick are waiting at the plane."

Walking across the tarmac beside Tad, Cindy felt conspicuous, almost like a celebrity, rescued by her own private bodyguard from the milling throng. She greeted Mr. Wainwright, then shook Mr. Resnick's hand shyly and found herself looking into the level eyes of a bald, muscular man only a couple of inches taller than her five feet six.

"Starting this late is deliberate," he told her

briskly. "We're going to skip the jayvee game and settle for the main event." Quickly she was hoisted into a seat next to Tad's and told to fasten her seat belt while the pilot twiddled the dials, adjusted his earphones, and began an unintelligible conversation with the airport tower.

"Hurry up to stand still," he told his passengers. "That's always the way."

Nevertheless, he turned the nose of the Cessna toward a line of small planes waiting for takeoff and patiently listened for instructions.

Cindy sat with tightly clasped hands, trying to quiet her pounding heart. "The minute we're up, you'll just love it," Tad told her comfortingly, and to her surprise, she did.

Downy clouds decorated the cold blue sky, and the little plane slid between them like a clever bird. The flying time was only about fifteen minutes, and most of it was over a metallic sea, empty except for a couple of fishing boats rolling in the swells. All pleasure craft were in dry dock for the winter.

The takeoff had been so effortless and smooth that Cindy was unprepared for a rather bumpy landing. She gasped, then laughed aloud. "That was wonderful," she shouted over Mr. Resnick's shoulder.

By the time they reached the football field, the jayvee contest had ended in a tie and the Homecoming Parade was starting. There were a couple of Model T Fords, a few more modern cars, and several flatbed trucks bearing the class floats, the Nantucket High School band, and finally the Homecoming Queen, who rode with her court of five girls, all of whom looked beautiful but chilly.

Cindy said with admiration, "Aren't they pretty!"

Tad glanced at the girls, then at Cindy. "I've seen prettier," he murmured too softly to be heard.

The green wooden grandstand on the east side of the field was already filled with Nantucket fans. Latecomers were standing three deep at either end. On a smaller set of bleachers opposite, the Vineyard rooters were making a din with air horns and cowbells. There were spectators of all ages in the stands—children in snowsuits; women in fur coats; bareheaded fathers with small boys riding piggyback on their shoulders; weather-beaten young fishermen with beards and long ponytails swinging from beneath knitted watch caps. Letting her eyes rove over the throng, Cindy picked out a number of Vineyard people with whom she was acquainted. A few waved their hands in recognition, but most had their eyes on the field.

As the teams ran out to the scuffed brown grass, the cheerleaders, Caroline included, led the onlookers in a rousing cheer. Her new outfit, in white and a purple brighter than the grapes that were the

Vineyard symbol, was very becoming. "See the second girl from the left?" said Cindy to Tad. "She's a very good friend of mine. The one you thought was a girl groom."

Caroline was behaving with all the enthusiasm her role demanded, jumping up and down, waving her crepe paper pom-poms, shouting the words of the school cheers at the top of her lungs. Not until the referees appeared in their zebra-striped tops and the supporters of both teams stood for the national anthem did Cindy's eyes return to the larger pageant about to unfold.

For her that is what it amounted to, a pageant. She cheered dutifully when Vineyard won the toss and whenever one of the players from the home team made a good play, but she saw the game more as a celebration than a serious contest. She thought of the Nantucket Whalers as friendly enemies who shared a tie that bound them together. Both teams were islanders.

Nantucket won the game, as was rather to be expected, because boys from the smaller school concentrated exclusively on football while the Vineyard supported a soccer team as well. The fans all stood up and cheered—for both sides, it seemed to Cindy—then folded their stadium blankets, stamped their feet to restore circulation, and moved off to airport buses or private cars.

At the bottom of the steps Cindy came across Caroline, who was clutching a coat thrown over her shoulders, and stopped to introduce her properly to Tad and the two older men. "Too bad we lost," Caroline said about the game, but she didn't seem overly concerned. She took time to give each of Cindy's escorts a winning smile. "Three men!" she cried. "Aren't you the lucky girl!"

Walking back from the bus to the plane, Mr. Wainwright was inclined to loiter, and Cindy stayed beside him as Tad and Jake Resnick strode on ahead. "That was a remarkable afternoon," he said reflectively. "Like stepping back in time to when small-town high school football was somehow *purer* than it is today. It's as though both teams knew that while it was a furious fight, it was still only a game."

"Is that so very different from mainland football?" Cindy asked.

Mr. Wainwright nodded. "But it's hard to say how. I kept thinking of the rivalry of Edgartown and Nantucket in the early days of whaling, when they were two of the richest seaports in the world. Did you feel a sense of nostalgia in the air?"

"No," Cindy had to confess. She didn't know quite what Mr. Wainwright was talking about. Perhaps he was only thinking aloud. Perhaps, like rich people, writers were different. She glanced up at her companion's face and found that he now looked amused.

"You're not much interested in football, are you, Cindy?"

"Not really." She added hastily, "But I loved coming with you today!"

"What do you like to do most in the world?"

Here was a question that Cindy could answer positively. "Ride horseback," she said.

"Ah!" Mr. Wainwright breathed deeply. "I should have guessed."

Then he tucked a hand under Cindy's elbow and hurried her along to the plane as he muttered to himself, "Poor Tad."

CHAPTER
7

ON SUNDAY MORNING CINDY was up at daybreak. Trying to avoid disturbing the rest of the family, she crept downstairs in woolen socks, carrying her riding boots. Quickly she ate two thick pieces of toast lavishly spread with homemade beach plum jam and drank a tall glass of milk. Hot cocoa would have tasted good, but she didn't want to waste time making it. She did, however, take time to leave a note on the kitchen blackboard: "Gone to the farm. Will be home in time for church. Cindy."

Except for the distant moan of a foghorn there was not a sound to be heard as she wheeled her bicycle out of the garage. The fields were still sleeping under a blanket of hoarfrost at this early hour. No rooster crowed, no gull screamed, no cars passed along the road Cindy traveled. She might have been the only person on earth.

However, by the time she reached Heatherfield, the sun was sending warm rays from beyond the sheltering hills. She raised her head in anticipation and drew in breaths of the cold air. It was bound to be a fine day.

Banner was not in his stall. Undoubtedly he was out in the field, where he occasionally spent the night when asthma threatened. Cindy picked up a saddle from the tack room and was starting down the back lane when Helen Park, wearing flannel pajamas, opened the farmhouse door. She was brushing her long hair and yawning.

"Hi, Cindy," she called sleepily. "I overslept."

"Hi, Mrs. Park. Is it okay if I ride first and then come back and help with the stable work?"

"Sure."

Cindy went on down to the fenced pasture at the foot of the incline. She whistled a summons, but Banner, usually so prompt to come to the gate, didn't even raise his head.

Something's wrong! Like the foghorn's danger signal, certainty raced to Cindy's brain. Had it been any other horse, she wouldn't have worried, but the black pony was different. He knew her. He liked her. He always came to her so gladly!

Dropping the saddle to the ground, Cindy didn't stop to open the gate. She climbed over it swiftly and ran to the spot where Banner stood. His head, usually held high, was drooping.

"You're hurt!"

A broad river of blood flowed from a horizontal gash in the pony's chest, and his head dropped even lower when Cindy came close. Immediately she saw a viscous fluid easing down Banner's right leg from a mangled knee. Shocked, she trembled and staggered back, afraid for the first time in her life that she might faint.

Then action replaced panic. Cindy raced for the farmhouse with all the speed her legs could command and flung herself through the door.

"Helen, come quick!" Tears gushed from her eyes and down her cheeks. "Banner's hurt! Terribly!"

Dragging a sweater over her head, Mrs. Park appeared in the upstairs hall. Even more than her ominous words, Cindy's use of her first name and her uncontrolled weeping struck Mrs. Park with foreboding. "What happened?"

"I don't know!" Cindy gasped. "I don't know! He's bleeding badly, and his leg could be broken." Recalling the pony's injuries, she squeezed her eyes shut, then opened them as Mrs. Park came running downstairs and brushed past her to get to the telephone.

Cindy sank down on the lowest step and tried to pull herself together. This was no time for hysterics. She cleared her streaming eyes with the back of her hands and swallowed the tears that dripped into her mouth.

Meanwhile, Mrs. Park was talking to the veterinarian. "Can you come right away? I'm afraid it's serious. We'll be down in the lower pasture with the pony." Turning from the phone, she tried to soothe Cindy's fears by telling her, "Dr. Shaw will be right over. He's a good guy, but I bet he's thinking accidents always happen on weekends."

Although she was fighting hard for self-control, Cindy couldn't seem to get to her feet until Mrs. Park took charge. "Get a blanket from the barn. I'll fetch a bucket of water and my first-aid kit." When she saw that Cindy's response was slow and dazed, she ordered, "Hurry, child!"

The brusque command brought Cindy out of shock. As she went out of the house, a part of her brain was nourished by the thought that she had been trusted. Mrs. Park hadn't waited to see for herself how badly Banner was hurt before calling the vet. She took a blanket from the pile in the tack room, choosing a lightweight one, and caught up with Mrs. Park on the lane, then ran ahead to open the gate.

Banner hadn't moved. Cindy knew why. He couldn't stand on his right hoof. She also knew what happened to a horse with a broken leg: a bullet or a lethal injection.

Don't let it happen to Banner, she prayed. Not to Banner!

Mrs. Park inspected the conspicuous chest wound, then saw the fluid easing down the pony's leg. "Dear God!" she whispered, reacting with horrified dismay. "Oh, you poor boy. You poor darling." To Cindy the uncharacteristic words sounded like a death sentence.

Cindy couldn't speak, but she didn't break down again. Without being told, she spread the blanket gently on Banner's back. The fear that chilled her to the very bone was greater than any emotion she had ever experienced.

Together the woman and girl stood beside the horse, waiting. How could such a terrible accident have happened? Cindy wondered, but investigation into the cause could come later. At this moment her concern was not for the how or why but for the victim, who could understand none of her words of attempted comfort but only the inflection of her voice.

Yet even when she talked to Banner softly, soothingly, his head did not lift or turn. He stayed in the same dejected posture until Dr. Shaw arrived in his old station wagon and managed to negotiate the stony path down the hill.

He was a bearded man, lithe and sinewy, and he wasted no time on greetings. "Hmm," he said when he saw the chest wound. "What did you do, fella, try to scale a barbed-wire fence?" Then he looked down, scowling grimly. "Bad news," he said. "The knee joint's punctured. Look at that." Indicating a triangle of hanging flesh, he motioned Helen Park toward his shoulder. "You can see all the way to the cannon bone."

"Are you telling me he'll have to be destroyed?" asked Mrs. Park with more courage than Cindy could comprehend. Weak and nauseated, Cindy leaned against the fence for support.

"There's certainly nobody on the island who can help him," said Dr. Shaw. "About all I can do is give him painkillers and antibiotics. We have no operating facilities."

"Is it possible to operate?" There was a slender ray of hope in Mrs. Park's voice.

"Possible, but surgery on such a puncture wound is always iffy."

"And expensive, I suppose?"

"Very."

"Where is the nearest horse hospital?"

"I'd suggest the Rochester Equine Center in New Hampshire."

New Hampshire? Cindy had never been to New Hampshire. It sounded as far away as New York City.

"Can we phone?" asked Mrs. Park.

"Of course, but consider the facts, Helen. Even if they can rustle up a surgical team on a Sunday, there's no promise an operation will be successful. Besides, just getting the pony there will require a lot of effort. And the cost may amount to several thousand dollars. Think carefully now. Is the pony worth it?"

Cindy gasped at the question, which sounded unfeeling, but Mrs. Park hesitated. "I'm under a lot of financial pressure right now," she admitted. "Perhaps I can raise a few hundred dollars, but no more."

"Do you own this horse?" asked Dr. Shaw.

Mrs. Park shook her head. "He belongs to Laurel Proctor, a girl from up-island. Her parents might help some, but they're not wealthy, and Laurel's off studying nursing in Boston."

"I think you've given me your answer."

"No!" Cindy gasped in spite of herself. She could have no part in this decision, but the cry came from a depth of feeling both adults recognized.

Mrs. Park looked from the veterinarian to the injured pony, and her hands clenched. "No," she repeated. "Banner is irreplaceable. He's great with the handicapped youngsters, and the 4-H kids adore him. He's a remarkable horse, and if it's at all possible, we're going to save him."

"And the money?"

"To hell with the money. We'll find it somewhere. Please call the hospital, Dr. Shaw."

"Very well, we'd better get going." Once the die was cast, Dr. Shaw looked relieved. "You're pretty remarkable yourself, Helen," he said. "I think you've made a brave decision."

Cindy would have stayed in the field with Banner had the vet not beckoned to her. "Come along with us. We'll need to find some way to rig up a makeshift splint."

First of all, however, came the long-distance call to New Hampshire. When Dr. Shaw turned away from the phone, he said, "They'll have an operating team standing by from four o'clock on. What time is it now?"

"Eight-fifteen."

"It's a four-hour drive from Woods Hole to the center," said the vet. "That should give us time enough." He turned to Cindy. "What's your name?"

"Cindy Foster."

"Can you use a saw?"

Cindy nodded. "My dad's a carpenter."

"Find a couple of old brooms, Cindy, and saw off the handles. Helen, we'll need two pillows, not feather pillows but foam rubber. Also, I'll want some very wide gauze. A roll or two of the widest the emergency room at the hospital can come up

with. That's closer to Heatherfield than our clinic."
He took a deep breath and continued as though he
were thinking aloud. "We'll need your horse trailer,
of course, with some extra padding—"

"Horse trailer?" Mrs. Park put her hands to her
cheeks. "It's off-island," she told him. "I rented it to
transport a stallion to a breeder in Pennsylvania.
By now it's probably somewhere in New Jersey."

"See if you can borrow one," said Dr. Shaw.

Under his competent direction the first stages of
the rescue operation got under way. Cindy had delivered the broomsticks and was mounting her bike,
ready to start off for the hospital in quest of bandages, when a young couple who were regular Sunday riders pulled into the parking space near the
barn. "One of the horses is badly hurt," she said
quickly. "Will you drive me to the hospital for some
supplies?"

On the way she explained the seriousness of the
situation, and of course Midge and Bill Henderson
offered to help. So did the resident in the emergency room, who was a horse lover and would be off
duty in another hour. Faith Bowman had come to
the hospital to visit a sick friend and now joined the
group. "I can take care of the stable work," she
promised.

The word spread by word of mouth and by telephone as Mrs. Park vainly tried to locate a horse

trailer. There were several other horse farms on the island, but Sunday morning was a bad time in which to locate the owners. Were they at church? Were they out riding? Or off-island for the weekend? Where could everybody be? When telephones weren't answered, Helen Park clenched her fists, looked at the clock, and tried another number.

Time dragged by. Cindy gritted her teeth and managed to help Bill Henderson and Dr. Shaw rig the splint and tape protective bandages against Banner's torn chest; but blood still seeped through, and his head still hung disconsolately. The clock crept toward ten, and still no trailer had been located. The situation was becoming desperate.

Then the resident doctor arrived from the hospital, offering a ray of hope. He had a friend in West Chop who kept a horse van on the island over the winter, along with a jeep to haul it. Henry Goldman and his family lived there only in the summer, but perhaps he could be reached at his home in Connecticut.

By now Mrs. Park was ready to jump at any possibility, no matter how remote. She turned over the house phone to the newcomer, who got the number from information, then dialed the Goldmans' Greenwich residence.

Cindy had been sent up to the house on an errand by Dr. Shaw, and arrived just in time to hear the

Vineyard end of the conversation.

"Henry? Eric Wynne. We've got some trouble on the island—an emergency—a badly injured horse. We need a trailer and we can't seem to locate one. Is yours available?

"Yes . . . sure, I understand. . . . No, of course not. . . ."

Was the answer negative? Cindy couldn't tell. Minutes passed, and finally Dr. Wynne hung up. "There's a trailer and a rig in Goldman's stable," he said, "but the keys are inside the house. We can use it, but he doesn't know any way we can get in short of breaking a window."

"For that we'll need the cooperation of the police," Mrs. Park said sensibly. "We can't leave the house unprotected."

"Dad could fix the window this afternoon!" Cindy proposed. "I know he'll be glad to do it."

"So long as you're not setting me up to rob a bank." Incredible as it seemed, Cindy's father stood in the doorway, her mother beside him. "We were just about to leave for church when we heard the bad news," Mrs. Foster said. "What can we do to help, Helen?"

"If we manage to get off, it will be a long trip to the hospital. You might make some sandwiches and pack a lunch basket."

As her mother moved toward the kitchen, more

people began to arrive. Word had crisscrossed the Vineyard as if borne on the wind, and the islanders rallied around like anxious neighbors. Soon a police car rolled in from the road, and Mr. Foster joined Dr. Wynne, climbing into the backseat. Cindy watched them speed off with the siren already shrilling.

"That's good," said Mrs. Park with a sigh of relief. "It'll be a short trip to West Chop." Even so, Cindy knew that they should reckon on at least an hour before the trailer could return to the farm, and it was already close to ten-thirty. When she ran back to the field and told Dr. Shaw that a van had been found, he seemed encouraged until she explained the situation in detail.

Then his expression changed. He looked grim. "We've got to make the noon boat." He added, with emphasis, "We've simply got to." Although his eyes remained on Banner, he said to Cindy, "Go up to the house and tell Helen to get the Steamship Authority to hold up the boat till we can get aboard."

Cindy gasped. "They'll never do that!"

"They'd better," Dr. Shaw replied firmly.

Cindy had never heard of a ferry schedule being tampered with. The boats plied back and forth from Woods Hole to either Vineyard Haven or Oak Bluffs with a regularity that didn't allow for any delay at either end. Not even a celebrity arriving or

leaving the island could hope for special considera-
tion.

Yet when Cindy delivered her message, Mrs.
Park didn't think such a request was beyond the
realm of possibility. She had just hung up from a
vain attempt to reach Laurel Proctor. Her parents
weren't at home, and there was no answer at the
Boston number she had been given. "Maybe Dr.
Shaw's name will carry more weight than mine
with the SSA. See if he can come up here, Cindy.
But don't leave Banner alone."

"Of course not!" Cindy stayed with the horse,
standing beside him in the field and stroking his
flank for more than half an hour. The ground was
cold, and so were her feet and hands. Even her
heart was chilled as she empathized with Banner's
suffering. And where was Laurel Proctor all this
time? "She'll be heartsick about this," Mrs. Park
had said. "Heartsick."

But she wasn't heartsick now. Cindy felt an un-
reasonable anger at Laurel welling in her breast. If
I owned Banner, she thought, I'd be here beside
him, not someplace a hundred miles away where
nobody could reach me. She fed her resentment to
relieve her own pain, then chided herself for such
behavior and tried to believe that this absent girl
could love Banner as much as she did.

From the Heatherfield entrance road strident

honks alerted the waiting islanders. Cindy glanced at her watch: eleven twenty-five. A small truck hitched to a horse trailer edged down the hill in low gear, while Dr. Shaw ran ahead to open the gate. Still standing beside Banner, Cindy called, "Are they holding the ferry?" She knew it was their only hope.

The veterinarian raised both hands in a gesture of uncertainty. "They said they'd try," he called back as Eric Wynne edged the truck through the narrow opening and brought the trailer as close as possible to the pony. He jumped down from the high seat, and the men opened the trailer door and lowered the ramp. Now came the hard part, persuading Banner to do his best to limp up it.

"Take his halter, Cindy. See if you can coax him," said Dr. Shaw. "No. Wait. Here comes Helen!"

But Mrs. Park shook her head. "Let Cindy try. He trusts her more than anyone—anyone but Laurel."

Murmuring words of encouragement, Cindy stood at Banner's head, pulling ever so gently on his halter. "Come, Banner. Good boy. Take just a step or two. You can make it."

Obediently the pony attempted to move forward, but when he tested his weight on the injured leg, he shrieked in pain, and in the end the men had to lift his heavy body and relieve some of the weight on his right foreleg. This took fifteen minutes. The ferry had already docked at Oak Bluffs, as everyone knew, and was now reloading. Time was running out.

Then a police car appeared on the scene, rocketing down the hill and swinging in a sharp U-turn, ready to start up again. "They're holding the boat!" the officer shouted. "Come on!"

There was no question of who would make the trip. Eric Wynne would drive his friend's truck. Mrs. Park and Dr. Shaw would squeeze into the cab beside him. The vet's medical kit and Mrs. Foster's picnic hamper were already stowed away, but at the last minute an extra pillow had to be found and tucked under Banner's right hoof.

To Cindy time seemed to move in slow motion, but finally they were off, a ragged cortege with the police car leading, siren screaming. Automobiles carrying many of the island helpers brought up the rear.

The ride to the dock took longer than usual, because it would be dangerous to jostle the pony, but on Banner's arrival at the ferry slip passengers gathered at the rail on the upper deck and cheered as the trailer was trundled aboard. Cindy and her parents stood on the bluff and watched the gangplank hauled back, the doors to the vehicle deck bang shut, and the boat pull out into the cold gray sound. "Well, that's that," Mr. Foster said. "I'd better get to fixing that window."

Without speaking, Cindy took a red scarf from around her neck and waved it, holding it high above her head, like a forlorn flag streaming in the winter wind.

"A banner for Banner," her mother said, putting an arm around Cindy's shoulders.

CHAPTER
8

NEVER HAD A SUNDAY seemed longer. In her imagination Cindy rode with Banner in the horse trailer, rumbling along for the many weary miles, wracked by the pain she knew he must be suffering. She shared his terror at the strange antiseptic smells of the hospital, flinched at the lights in the operating room, shuddered at the thought of the needle containing anesthetic.

"Darling, try to eat a little chicken," her mother said at dinner. Cindy shook her head and pushed her plate away.

"The window's fixed. Everything's secure at

Goldman's place. There's nothing else we can do."
Her father's words were sympathetic, understanding but not comforting.

Peter sat and kicked his feet against the rungs of his chair. Not being able to think of something pertinent to say, he said nothing.

When darkness fell, Cindy brought her neglected homework to the kitchen table and sat under the overhead light staring at the unopened books in front of her. In the living room the rest of the family sat in front of the TV watching a PBS program.

At seven o'clock the telephone rang, and Cindy leaped to answer it. Helen Park was phoning from New Hampshire. "We'll be starting home shortly," she said. "The surgeon was on hand, as promised, and they've started the operation, but of course they can't promise it will be successful. The knee's in rough shape, they say, but there's some good news. The cannon bone isn't broken."

"When will they know about the operation?" Cindy asked.

"Four or five days from now, the surgeon says." Mrs. Park made a sound more like a snort than a chuckle. "Whether Banner lives or dies I've got to come up with some three thousand dollars."

Three thousand dollars! It sounded like a fortune to Cindy, as it certainly must to Mrs. Park. Where would it come from? How could she possibly raise such a sum? Borrow from the bank?

Lying in bed that night, Cindy was mulling over the money problem when a possible answer occurred to her. What about the 4-H group? All the girls loved the pony, as did the children who were learning to ride. No horse in Heatherfield Farm was more popular than Banner, none sweeter, more responsive, more admired.

Suppose, just suppose, that she and the other girls could organize a campaign to raise money for the hospital bill, not the entire amount—that seemed unrealistic—but enough to make a substantial difference to Helen Park. Cindy was too bone tired to work out the details, but she promised herself to think about it in the morning.

Actually, during breakfast and the bus ride to school, she thought about little else. Cindy wasn't especially ambitious, nor was she politically minded. She had never been nominated for class office and was considered something of a loner, but now "that girl who's interested in horses" had a cause.

First she made an appointment with the 4-H Club leader and enlisted her support. Then, at lunchtime, she tackled the girls in the horsemanship group and impressed upon them the importance of raising money—a great deal of money!—for a reason that was inevitably dear to their hearts. Later she cut math class and phoned the *Vineyard Gazette,* the island's weekly newspaper, asking to speak to a reporter. She felt daring and grown-up when she placed the call, but when a man's deep voice came on the line, she became uncertain, even tremulous.

Perhaps Cindy's trepidation made the man listen, and listen closely. "Yeah," he said, "could make a good feature story. Got any pictures of this horse?"

"D'you mean photographs or snapshots?"

"Either one."

"You might try Mrs. Park. She owns Heatherfield Farm. Or the Proctors from up-island. They're Laurel Proctor's parents. Banner belongs to Laurel, you see."

The reporter sighed as though justifiably confused. "Why can't the Proctors come up with the money?" he asked.

"Three thousand dollars?" Cindy's voice rose several octaves. "Are you kidding? They're not *rich!*"

There was a moment's silence on the other end of the line. Then the man said patiently, "I'd better take a run out to the farm and straighten this out."

"When?" asked Cindy.

"Can't say exactly. I may make it this afternoon, but if not, I'll get to it before Thursday."

"Thanks ever so much, Mr. . . . ."

"Lowell. Mark Lowell."

Thursday was Thanksgiving, and the *Gazette* came out every Friday, so the reporter had made a virtual promise that Banner's story would appear in the next issue. Now she had to alert Mrs. Park, whom she had not yet consulted about her money-raising plan because she wanted to present it as an accomplished fact. Had she been too brash, too quick to assume such a lot of responsibility?

It was too late to worry about that now. Cindy fed the last of her change into the slots of the pay telephone. "Helen?" Again Mrs. Park's first name burst forth spontaneously.

"Yes, Cindy."

"Listen, I've had a great idea, and if you agree, it just may work!" Enthusiastically Cindy sketched out her plan and the success she had met in enlisting the help of the 4-H group. "Besides that," she said, "Mark Lowell, a reporter on the *Gazette*, is going to come to see you."

"Cindy, slow down! You sound as out of control as a runaway horse. This isn't like you."

"I know, Helen, but you will talk to Mr. Lowell, won't you?"

"I'll talk to him, sure." Mrs. Park's voice sounded tired. "But stop barging ahead until you get Laurel's approval of this scheme. She owns Banner. I just board him."

"So who will have to pay the hospital bill, Laurel or you?"

"I took the responsibility," Mrs. Park admitted, "without her permission. Cindy, it's important that you get in touch with Laurel."

"Does she know about Banner's accident?"

"Yes, she knows. I was able to reach her before we left New Hampshire. She was devastated, of course."

"Why couldn't I just call the Proctors?"

"Because Banner is Laurel's horse, Cindy."

Reluctantly, because she was afraid Laurel might consider her too officious, Cindy put in a long-distance call to Boston from home as soon as evening rates went on, and a girl's voice said, "Yes, this is Laurel Proctor."

"My name is Cindy Foster. I ride—rode—Banner a lot this fall. I'm terribly sorry about his accident."

"So am I." Laurel's voice sounded dull, defeated.

Trying to think logically and sound more organized than she felt, Cindy explained the reason for her call. "The 4-H group would take responsibility. You wouldn't be involved at all, but Mrs. Park wants me to get your permission." Once the words were out, Cindy knew she had sounded ungracious.

Laurel, however, seemed not to notice. "Go

ahead," she acquiesced. "Helen can't raise the money, and neither can I. Banner was a present for my eighteenth birthday, and my father made it plain that the pony was mine to take care of from that time on." Before hanging up, she added, "Even if you bring in a couple of hundred dollars, it will be a big help."

Two hundred? By now Cindy was aiming for a thousand. She said as much to her mother, who was paying household bills at a desk in the living room.

Mrs. Foster, who had heard about Cindy's project, looked faintly skeptical. "You'd better start keeping track of your expenses," she said. "That includes telephone calls."

"I will, Mom," Cindy promised. She wanted to appear businesslike, although this detail must not get in the way of her major objective. All evening she sat and made notes on a pad of paper. If she seemed to be absorbed in her homework, so much the better. Homework was another detail that could wait.

Inevitably Banner kept tugging at the fringes of her concentration. Banner with his eyes clear and his head high. Banner trotting, cantering, galloping, completely well again. Perhaps raising funds would assure his recovery. She was too involved to see this as wishful thinking.

The next morning Cindy met Caroline on the way

to the bus and realized that she had missed her on Monday. "Where were you yesterday?" she asked.

"Home in bed with a fever. I caught a cold. The game was worth it, though."

The game? Saturday had become hazy. "Caro, have you heard about Banner?"

"What about him?" asked Caroline irritably. "I told you I've been sick."

With graphic intensity, Cindy told her about finding the pony streaming blood and unable to walk. She described the hunt for a horse trailer, the race to the ferry, the anxiety with which they all were waiting for news of the operation. "Oh, the poor baby! Oh, the poor dear," Caroline said sympathetically. "I wish there were something I could do."

"There is," Cindy replied at once. "We're going to try to raise money for Banner's hospital bill. Will you help?"

"Of course, I'll help. That is, if it doesn't take up too much time. I'm in the Christmas pageant at church, you know, and the skating rink is opening next week, and—"

"Caro, don't you *care* about Banner?"

Cindy didn't expect a candid answer. Caroline cared, but not enough. Not the way I care, Cindy thought sadly. "Well, save any time you can spare," she said without rebuke. "We're going to need you."

"Oh, I will," promised Caroline as the bus turned into the school drive. "I will!" She sounded relieved to have been let off so lightly.

Cindy walked off to put her jacket in her locker with a feeling that the cement of her friendship with Caroline was being chipped away even further. Their paths had separated. What Cindy considered an all-important crusade was to Caroline just another extracurricular activity.

After her morning classes Cindy ate a hurried lunch and was on time for an appointment she had dared make with the high school principal. Perhaps if she could enlist his support . . .

Busy with a dozen more urgent problems, Ronald Dickson listened to Cindy's story with sympathy, but when she said, "I thought maybe if each homeroom teacher could read an announcement and the whole school knew about how much money it's going to take—" he shook his head.

"We're not in the money-raising business, Cynthia," Mr. Dickson said, then softened his refusal with a smile. "Try some of the charitable organizations on the island." When she rose to leave, Cindy felt certain she could read his mind. One injured horse. Three thousand dollars? The girl's not thinking straight.

As she closed the door of the principal's office behind her, Tad, who was headed down the hall, accosted her. "Naughty, naughty," he said teasingly.

"Are you expelled or just suspended?"

Cindy didn't smile. "Oh, Tad, a terrible thing has happened. Banner's been hurt, badly. He's in a horse clinic on the mainland, and they don't know whether he'll live or die. But in any case, it's going to cost thousands of dollars."

Tad whistled sympathetically. "Who's paying?"

"That's the big question." Cindy explained the situation and added with a feeble smile, "Horses should have accident insurance just like people."

"So what's going to happen now?"

"We're going to try to raise at least part of the money." Cindy lifted her chin firmly.

"Let me be the first to contribute." Tad spoke lightly, but his eyes were compassionate as he pulled a wallet from the pocket of his jeans and thrust a bill into Cindy's hand.

Looking down, she saw at once her telephone number scribbled in ink along one margin. This was the bill he had written on the day they had met, and he had kept it all this time. As Cindy managed to conquer her surprise and thank him, Tad explained awkwardly, "I won't need it anymore. I know the number by heart."

Cindy was touched. "You're sure you want to?"

"I'm sure. By now I've got a pretty good idea of how much that pony means to you." He spoke with perception, almost with tenderness as he watched

Cindy fold the bill carefully and put it in her pocket. "This is very sweet of you, Tad," she said in a whisper.

Suddenly, just as the warning bell rang for fifth period, Tad's usual composure reasserted itself. "We're off to New York for Thanksgiving, but there's a great movie coming to Edgartown next week. How about going next Saturday night? Okay?"

"Okay," Cindy murmured with a quick nod. What a friendly, understanding guy!

"I'll call you," Tad said as he pounded down the hall at a run.

The Thanksgiving holiday was cut short this year by a state requirement Cindy only vaguely understood. After the usual family celebration she returned to school on Friday still feeling desolate about Banner. Mrs. Park hadn't yet received an encouraging word from the doctors, although she considered this not unusual. Cindy, on the other hand, was filled with impatience that she could scarcely control. She went to her regular morning classes but kept shifting in her seat nervously because she knew that the *Vineyard Gazette* was already on the street and she was eager to see what sort of space Banner's story had been given.

Right after lunch she went to the school library, and there on the checkout desk was the folded newspaper, with Banner's two-column picture on the front page. Cindy gasped in delight. ISLANDERS RALLY TO SAVE PONY'S LIFE, read the headline.

"Friend of yours?" asked the librarian.

"Yes. Oh, yes!" Cindy stood reading with complete absorption. "Thank you," she murmured when she had finished, then wandered off in a trance. Mark Lowell had written a wonderful, warm article about Banner. He *understood*!

Cindy was assured that word of Banner's plight would spread across the island. Everybody read the *Gazette,* and the story, while not sentimental, was emotional enough to tug at heartstrings. This might be the boost needed to get the fund-raising campaign under way.

The girls on the newly formed committee agreed. They met at the farm that afternoon and appropriated Mrs. Park's living room as an office. "Let's make a list of all the horse farms on the island and all the people we know who own horses and are likely to contribute," Cindy suggested. "We'll divide it up, and tonight and tomorrow we can start phoning."

Each of the group left having promised to do her part, and Cindy's optimism was restored. She even hummed a tune on the way home and went into the house with eyes shining. "Mom, have you seen the *Gazette*?"

"I have indeed. Mark wrote a really sensitive piece."

"Do you know him?"

"I know his parents. Mark's been off at college for the past few years. A journalism major, I think. He's young to be on the *Gazette* staff." Opening her favorite cookbook, Mrs. Foster put on her reading glasses and looked up a recipe, then glanced up in mild annoyance as the telephone rang. "Cindy, will you get it?"

"Cynthia?" asked a man's voice, vaguely familiar.

"Yes."

"This is Ronald Dickson speaking. I've just read the *Gazette* story on that horse you were telling me about."

"Yes?"

"Well, it so happens there's a five minute slot open at a special assembly I'm calling for Tuesday."

"Oh, wonderful! Would you—"

"Just a minute, Cynthia. I've been thinking that if you were to make a personal appeal, it might be effective."

"Me?" Dropped into that five-minute slot like a coin into a vending machine? Cindy shuddered at the thought. "I can't talk to the whole school, Mr. Dickson. I've never made a speech in my life!"

"It's never too soon to learn," said the high school principal, using one of his many clichés. "Think it over, Cynthia. You can let me know on Monday morning what you decide."

"Mom, I can't. I just can't!" wailed Cindy after she had hung up. "Even reading something aloud in English class gives me the jitters."

"You won't be reading. You'll be speaking—about something close to your heart."

Too close, Cindy thought. "What if I start to cry?"

"You won't. You have too much self-control."

"Maybe if I write it all out—" Even while protesting, Cindy knew that this was something, no matter how terrifying, that she would have to do for Banner's sake. She couldn't refuse.

CHAPTER
9

CINDY SAT ON ONE of the three chairs placed at the back of the platform, her clammy hands clasped in her lap. The auditorium, although small by mainland standards, seemed vast and unfamiliar. The faces of the student body were a blur.

Mr. Dickson was reading the usual announcements, making an occasional jolly comment, unconcerned that she was dying, her heart ready to stop.

"... in a slight break from routine ... Cynthia Foster has something special to say to you." The principal was turning, actually smiling, walking away from the podium, which looked as solid as a tombstone. How could she possibly get to her feet when her knees felt as slippery as tapioca pudding? How could she take the necessary four or five steps?

Cindy's mouth was dry, her expression agonized as she staggered forward and gripped the corners of the slanting shelf with her hands. She looked down at the card filled with careful notes and couldn't read her own writing. Only the word BANNER, printed in capital letters, stood out.

Cindy took a long breath and leaned forward. "I'm here to tell you a true story about a pony," she squeaked, "a wonderful pony named Banner who lives at Heatherfield Farm."

Gradually her voice grew stronger, because she wanted to reach the people out there, this faceless audience, her schoolmates, and tell them how extraordinary the black pony was, how important to the children in the handicapped program, how gentle they found him, how responsive. "Banner is one of a hundred horses that live on this island," she said. "He may be the brightest and the best. At least that's what the children think.

"Saturday night a week ago, out in the field, Banner was hurt, badly. Nobody's sure how it happened, but he may have been gored by a boar who got in through a break in the fence. I happened to be the one to find him," she said, and described his injuries graphically, wanting to share her concern.

"The veterinarian, Dr. Shaw, said the pony's only chance for survival was to be sent to an off-island hospital.

"Banner had to be operated on at the earliest possible time," Cindy continued. "All sorts of people—people we didn't know—helped get him there. They borrowed a horse trailer and held up the noon ferry for fifteen minutes in order to get him aboard."

How long had she been talking? Cindy wondered. How long had everyone been so attentive? She went on, "It was like a soap opera, sort of," she continued. "Only Banner is *real*! And he isn't out of danger, even though the operation is over. He's still being kept at the hospital in a padded cell." She flushed as laughter rippled across the room. "I mean, a padded *stall*!

"All this is costing thousands of dollars, and nobody knows where the money is coming from—yet. Banner is very special. So are the folks who live on this island. Maybe we can find a way to help."

Afterward Cindy couldn't remember a word she had actually spoken. As the kickoff for a money-raising campaign it had been a soft sell. She had no conception of how to get people to reach into their pockets or purses for a worthy cause. All she had done was to try to touch their feelings and hope that generosity would follow.

Nothing might have come of her little speech if the Associated Press had not followed up the *Gazette* story and flown a Boston reporter to the island. Always keen to handle a good human-interest yarn, Samantha Jones interviewed Mrs. Park, Dr. Shaw, two of the children in the handicapped riding program, and finally Cindy herself, showing up at school in midafternoon on Thursday.

Sitting at a table in a quiet corner of the school library, Cindy for the second time told Banner's story, explaining the urgent need to raise funds.

"How are you going to go about it?" the reporter asked. Looking as young as a college student, she had straight brown hair that fell forward over her cheeks, and her hazel eyes searched Cindy's disconcertingly.

"I'm not sure," Cindy confessed, "but now the whole school knows—" She stopped short as she saw the dubious expression on Samantha's face.

"You think somebody else may pick up the ball and run with it? That won't happen. You started this thing, Cindy. You've got to see it through."

"But how?" Aside from phoning island horse farms and horse owners, Cindy hadn't been thinking ahead to the complex mechanics of getting people to donate.

"For starters, you might get the *Gazette* to publish an address to which contributions can be sent.

Then I'd alert the grammar school children, who love to get involved in projects. After all, the handicapped riders come from that group, not the high school crowd. If I were running this show, I'd have platoons of them out every Saturday morning until Christmas at the supermarkets and on the main streets of Edgartown and Oak Bluffs and Vineyard Haven. Set them up with tin cans with slots in the top. Then find some special giveaway gimmick to attract passersby, like the red paper flowers the veterans use every spring."

"Maybe miniature banners?"

"Great! The little kids could color them in school." Samantha glanced at her watch. "I've got to get going, or I'll miss my plane. Good luck, Cindy, and keep in touch. You can call me collect at the Boston office if you have any exciting news."

Cindy had never met anyone quite like Samantha Jones, crisp, efficient, yet warmly sympathetic to Banner's plight. She told her family about the interview while they were having dinner and realized that Peter had put down his fork and was listening to every word she said.

"I could help," he suggested when Cindy paused for breath. "I could be chairman of a fifth-grade committee."

The offer was unexpected, but Cindy reacted swiftly. "Why not? That's really nice of you, Peter.

Let's organize it over the weekend, okay? I'm loaded with homework tonight."

"Speaking of the weekend," Mrs. Foster said, "Tad Wainwright phoned and wants you to call him back."

"Will do," Cindy promised, and added by way of explanation, "We're going to the movies Saturday night."

"You mean, you've got a *date* with Tad?" Peter commented.

"Not a real date, silly. Just the movies."

Cindy reached for the telephone as soon as she had helped clear the table, but an incoming call interrupted. "Cindy? Helen Park. I'm going to drive with Laurel and her mother up to see Banner on Saturday. Want to go along?"

Did she want to go along? Cindy's heart leaped. "Oh, that's wonderful!" she cried. "What time?"

"We're planning to make the nine o'clock ferry from Vineyard Haven. Can you meet us there?"

"Of course!"

Cindy put the receiver down on the cradle softly, as though a loud noise might break the spell. She was going to New Hampshire on Saturday. With shining eyes she told her mother the good news.

"That's lovely, Cindy, but what about Tad?"

"What *about* Tad? A movie isn't such a big deal. I'll just tell him I can't go."

With a sigh Mrs. Foster said, "Do it gently, dear. Tad's a nice boy."

Preoccupied, Cindy scarcely heard her. She riffled the pages of the telephone directory until she came to *W*, then remembered that the Wainwrights' number, being a new one, wouldn't be in the book. While she was dialing information, her mother looked at her in mild astonishment. "You don't even know his number?" she said, shaking her head.

"Tad? Cindy. Mom says you called."

"Yeah," Tad replied. "By the way, that was some speech."

"Do you mean it was okay or terrible? I've never been so scared."

"It was good." After this brief praise, Tad's manner became teasing. "Maybe you should go on television." Then he became serious again. "What time shall I pick you up on Saturday night?"

"Oh, Tad, I should have told you right away. I can't go to the movies. You see, we're going up to New Hampshire to see Banner, and I'm sure we won't be back in time."

There was silence on the other end of the line.

"I'm sorry," Cindy said.

"I'm sorry, too." Tad's voice was flat. He sounded disappointed, but Cindy knew she had made the right—the only!—decision.

"Give me a raincheck," she suggested before hanging up.

Then she sat biting her lower lip for a minute. "I can't understand why he sounded so annoyed," she told her mother. "We can go to the movies anytime but I can't turn down a chance to see Banner!"

"Perhaps it's you, not the movie, that Tad wants to see."

Cindy frowned. "Oh, come on, Mom!" Only a few years ago her mother had been saying, "Why don't you try to make more *girl*friends?" and now she was doing an about-face and promoting this *boy*!

Her mother read Cindy's expression correctly. "Things will probably sort themselves out," she said with a shrug. "But sometimes you act like sixteen-going-on-twelve."

Cindy spent Friday in a daze of anticipation. Early in the evening she chose the clothes she would wear to New Hampshire and put them on a chair beside her bed. Should she wash her hair and blow-dry it? Yes, she decided, thankful for once that she wore her brown hair in natural short curls. As she stood in the shower, she wondered what Laurel Proctor would be like.

About Mrs. Proctor she didn't wonder at all, so she was pleased to find her both pleasant and cordial when they met the next morning. A slight, small-waisted woman, she wore her gray-streaked red hair in a bun on top of her head and had eyes of a deep gray that matched the color of the sound. "Helen has told me about all your help," she said. "Laurel and I really appreciate it."

Mrs. Proctor was driving her own car, a small Buick station wagon with a good many miles on it. She and Mrs. Park sat in the front seat, and Cindy was put in the rear with a picnic lunch stowed away in the luggage space behind her. Once the car had been parked carefully on the ferry, all three went up on deck, but as soon as the captain pulled away from the dock, a chill wind sent them below again.

The trip across Vineyard Sound seemed long to Cindy. It always did. And today she was anxious to get on the road to New Hampshire. She was told they would pick up Laurel at a bus stop near Route 3, on the outskirts of Boston, and while the women chatted in the front seat, Cindy could scarcely control her impatience.

Mrs. Proctor drove well and quickly. After the Sagamore Bridge over the Cape Cod Canal the highways were broad and the traffic was light, but the first hundred miles passed slowly. The road skirted a number of small Massachusetts towns before joining Route 128, where great industrial complexes faced one another across a superhighway. Huge buildings with impressive names—Polaroid, Raytheon, Honeywell—dwarfed the cars speeding along below them and made Cindy feel small and unsure. Now she understood why it was often hard for Vineyard natives to go to college off-island. "Going to the United States," they called it jokingly. Indeed, this seemed a foreign country to Cindy. She peered through the window apprehensively, glad that she lived on the Vineyard.

Mrs. Proctor arrived at the bus stop just before noon, and Laurel came running across the paved parking area as soon as she saw her mother's car. Her red hair was streaming in the wind, her cheeks were rosy, and she looked even more self-assured than the girl Cindy remembered.

"Let's put a few more miles under our wheels," suggested Mrs. Proctor after embracing her daughter and introducing Cindy. "Then we'll stop in a rest area and have a tailgate lunch."

"Would you like to sit with your mother?"

Helen Park opened the door at her side and prepared to get out, but Laurel said, "No, I'll sit with Cindy," and climbed into the backseat.

Cindy stared straight ahead, overcome by a reaction to Laurel's presence that was hard to control. Here was the girl to whom Banner belonged, as he would never belong to her. Resentful, she tried to conquer emotions she knew were foolish, but she couldn't seem to utter a word or turn her face and smile. She was sure—absolutely sure!—that Laurel didn't love the black pony nearly as much as she did.

After about a minute Laurel spoke. "You found Banner after he was hurt. Can you tell me about it?"

Cindy shook her head.

"I understand. It must have been awful."

Cindy nodded.

"Since I've been in nursing school I've had to face a lot of things that were hard, but if I'd been in your place a year ago, I'm sure I'd have fainted."

"I almost did." Cindy knew that she spoke bitterly, but she couldn't help it.

After a long silence Laurel began to talk softly. "I remember the day I got Banner. I'd always wanted a horse of my own more than anything, and my parents had given me a check—a big one!—to spend any way I wanted.

"I didn't know a thing about horses then—except how to ride one. I couldn't even put on a saddle or bridle without help." Laurel gave a reminiscent sigh.

"There was nothing for sale on the Vineyard at the time, but of course I was wildly impatient, and I went to a dealer I'd heard about on the mainland—in Taunton—and told him I was looking for an eight-year-old mare. He didn't have one, but he brought out this black pony."

Laurel paused. "I didn't know that you should never look at a horse's face, only at his conformation."

"Why not?" Cindy was forced to ask.

"Because you don't want to fall in love with him."

"Is that what happened to you?"

"Of course."

"Me, too. The minute I saw him, with those eyes and that expression—" Cindy broke off and closed her lips tightly. She hadn't expected to be drawn into saying so much.

"He was brought to the island in a truck," Laurel continued. "The deliveryman led him out and handed me the rope. I had bought a book called *How to Take Care of a Horse,* and we put him in a little one-stall horse barn in the fenced field behind our house. Banner lived there for a year, and I rode him every day." Suddenly, in a cry from the heart, Laurel said, "You don't know how much I miss him!"

Cindy turned and looked at the girl sitting beside her—really looked at her—studying her face for the first time: high cheekbones; a generous mouth; pale eyebrows lightly penciled; eyes that looked into Cindy's with sorrowful intensity.

Helen Park turned from the front seat and said, "Tell Cindy how bad he was at first."

"Bad? I don't believe it."

"Oh, he was very naughty!" Laurel told her with a chuckle. "The book told me all the right things to do: to treat him with respect; to try to win his confidence rather than scold him, even if he became grumpy or annoyed. What the author didn't say was what to do if he got loose and ran away."

"He ran away?"

"Several times. The police scanner would pick him up and report there was a black horse running down Music Street in West Tisbury. Music Street of all places! Right off the main road! Other times he'd show up at somebody's farm in the hills or be seen trotting along a dirt track toward the beach."

"I told you," called Mrs. Park to Cindy, "he wasn't always so biddable."

"But he was smart!" Laurel said proudly. "When I bought Banner, he was really in kindergarten—didn't even know his aids. I had to teach him everything about how to behave, but I must say he was a fast learner."

At this point Mrs. Proctor began to slow down. "There's a rest area ahead," she interrupted. "Anybody hungry?"

CHAPTER

10

AFTER LUNCH MRS. PARK moved into the backseat of the car with Cindy, and Laurel sat up front with her mother. Each pair talked privately as the station wagon sped along a few miles over the speed limit.

Cindy alternately glanced at her watch and gazed at the rocky landscape studded with bare trees. During quiet intervals she did some serious thinking. Helen had been right. Laurel's love for Banner glowed in her eyes, softened her voice when she talked about him. How helpless she must have felt when he was injured, forced to depend on others when she must have longed to be with him.

Any lingering feeling of envy for the older girl's ownership of the pony drained away as the remaining miles were covered.

"I thought you two would get along." Mrs. Park spoke as though she could read Cindy's mind.

Cindy nodded. "She's a great person, but do you think she realizes how enormous the hospital bills are going to be?"

"She knows, but she's not putting the cart before the horse, so to speak. If Banner survives—"

"Don't say 'if,' " objected Cindy. "He'll get well. I *know* he will."

One of the veterinarians on the operating team was on hand to talk to the visitors and show them the X rays. "You can see the deep rupture in the joint capsule clearly," he said. "The operation took more than three hours, a long time to keep a horse anesthetized. We had to clean the wound, remove broken chips of cartilage, and close the joint."

Laurel looked closely at the pictures, but Cindy held back. She longed to see Banner, not listen to surgical talk. "The pony came out of anesthesia in a padded recovery room where we keep postoperative patients. He thrashed about so desperately we had to give him strong sedatives, and we still don't know whether he did any harm to the knee. One thing's sure. We'll have to keep him for another week or so."

"Thank you, Doctor. May we see him now?" Laurel spoke with a composure Cindy felt she could never achieve.

"Certainly. Please follow me."

Banner was in a very clean stall. His right hoof was encased in a ball of safety wadding, and his leg was bandaged thickly to above the injured knee. Laurel, who had gone ahead with the doctor, approached the pony slowly. In a voice almost too low for Cindy to hear she said, "Banner."

The horse pricked up his ears, although he didn't raise his head in greeting. Laurel moved closer and stroked his bent neck. "My sweet Banner," she crooned. The pony's head lifted slightly and turned toward Laurel, but he didn't attempt to move.

Cindy could see his lusterless eyes. Where had the shine gone? He looked ill and dispirited, unable to understand why he was here; but he knew his owner's voice. There was no doubt of that. And Laurel stayed with him for a long time, stroking him gently and offering him the comfort of her presence, the only meaningful gift she could give.

When Laurel finally moved away, the two women urged Cindy forward, but she shook her head. She needed time to swallow the lump in her throat and blink back the tears that stood in her eyes. Laurel hadn't cried. Nor must she!

Fighting for self-control, she stood breathing

deeply, carefully, when there flashed into her mind
the memory of a wondrous sunset ride on a brisk
November day, when the lagoon was glowing and
the sky was beribboned with pink and orange. She
and Banner had made their way along a sandy
shore scalloped with seaweed, and she had watched
the sun drop like an orange ball below the distant
trees. Smoke drifted from chimneys as lights began
to go on in scattered houses. A pair of mallards rose
almost at Banner's hooves, but he didn't flinch.
What a lovely time that had been!

Helen Park touched Cindy's arm. "Your turn
now," she said with an encouraging smile.

Cindy stepped quietly forward, resisting an impulse to walk on tiptoe, as if she were entering a
hospital room. "Banner," she whispered. "Banner,
remember me?"

The pony turned his head and nickered softly.
The deep inverted commas of his nostrils twitched
as they caught her scent. Painfully he managed to
bear his weight on his injured leg and come toward
her. Cindy reached out to touch his forelock and
looked deep into his eyes, which today were the
color of black tea. In an open hand she offered him
the apple that had been a lump in her jacket pocket
all the way from home. His nose dipped forward
into Cindy's palm, and she could feel his breath on
her fingers as he lipped the fruit gently and took it

into his mouth. Then, chewing, he regarded her for a long minute.

What was he thinking about? Cindy wondered. Was he reminded of happy canters along woodland paths, the fragrance of drenched earth after a thunderstorm? "You're coming home soon," Cindy assured him. "You're going to be all right."

Her father was already at the table, contentedly reading the Sunday paper, when Cindy came down to breakfast the next morning. Once a week he indulged himself by buying the *Boston Globe*. "Morning, dear," he said as she poured herself some orange juice. "How was yesterday?"

"Long," Cindy replied with a yawn. "Banner has to stay in the hospital for more time than they thought."

"Is the leg healing?"

"They hope so." Compulsively Cindy yawned again.

"Here's something to wake you up." Her father passed a section of the newspaper across the table. There, looking up at her from the page, was another picture of Banner. Laurel, radiant, was beside him, holding his bridle. She was wearing riding clothes, and there were leaves on the trees behind her. She was looking happy and proud.

Under the by-line of Samantha Jones the feature

article that followed was amazingly complete. Samantha described the pony as though she actually knew him. She called him "irreplaceable" because of his patience with the handicapped children of Martha's Vineyard, praised the islanders for their rescue operation, wrote in detail of the events of that remarkable Sunday, and ended by saying that Banner was still not out of the woods, that medical bills were still mounting, that antibiotics alone cost a hundred dollars a day.

How the reporter got this last piece of information Cindy could only guess, but even her brief acquaintance with Samantha made her suspect she had called the hospital. She wasn't a young woman to leave many stones unturned. She must also have phoned Mrs. Park, because in the very last paragraph she wrote, "A special fund has been established. Contributions may be sent to Banner himself." There followed a post office box number with the address of Heatherfield Farm.

"Wow!" Cindy breathed when she had finished reading. "This is really something."

"It's a darned good story," her father agreed. "And the timing couldn't be better. The AP reaches newspapers all over the country, and a Sunday feature with this much appeal is bound to be read."

"Will it bring in some money, do you think?" Cindy asked seriously.

Her father's eyes twinkled. "I wouldn't be surprised."

By the end of the day the island buzzed with news of the AP coverage. A group of adults banded together and offered their services, and early the next week the Banner Fund, as it came to be called, was swept out of Cindy's hands and organized on a basis the 4-H Club considered very professional.

A realtor negotiated the loan of a vacant office; a businessman contributed a temporary telephone. Two young men brought an old desk and a couple of chairs from the Vineyard Haven Thrift Shop, and a high school teacher furnished a portable typewriter.

Cindy felt enormously relieved. As her father put it, she'd had a tiger by the tail, and she couldn't have held on much longer. Not that she didn't work hard—as hard as even those who had far more time to contribute. And she didn't shirk her chores at the farm because she knew Helen Park was similarly burdened.

With Thanksgiving a memory and Christmas in the air, the children in the handicapped group came for their final lesson in the winter program. On this special day some of their mothers came with them, to witness their progress or lend their support. All the 4-H helpers were on hand, along with the volunteers, and Cindy was holding the long line of a big, amenable gelding named Ben while one of the instructors helped an autistic boy to mount.

For a long time Herbert had refused to even go near a horse, but after weeks of encouragement he became able to sit in the saddle and allow himself to be led around the practice ring. Herbert was still withdrawn. He seldom spoke a word, but when he saw Cindy, his lips started to tremble and he looked around in confusion.

Attempting to calm him, Cindy moved closer and stroked the gelding's chestnut coat. "Big Ben, nice Ben," she said softly. "Ben likes you, Herbert."

The child could not be assuaged. He shook his head violently and finally managed to croak, "Where's Banner?"

"He'll be back soon," Cindy told him. "When you come in the spring, he'll be here. You can go riding on him then."

Herbert gave a sigh of either anticipation or disappointment and settled down, allowing Ben to be led around at a walk. The mothers and the volunteers applauded, but Herbert did not venture a smile.

Nevertheless, Helen Park was delighted. "That was a real breakthrough," she said to Cindy. "You could tell Herbert made the connection between you and Banner. You could see he cared."

Others asked after the pony they called the Black Stallion, and when they discovered Mrs. Park and Cindy had gone to New Hampshire and seen him, they seemed pleased. Several of the children had brought handmade get-well cards, and when they all trooped up to the farmhouse for a farewell party, they viewed their handiwork with pride. The climax of the afternoon came when one of the mothers handed the 4-H leader an envelope.

"I don't know whether this should go to you or Mrs. Park," she said, "but we all want to do something for your wonderful pony." The check inside, for a hundred dollars, was made out to the Banner Fund.

Cindy was well aware that most of the parents of these handicapped kids had to struggle to make ends meet. Wealthier people usually sent their children off-island to private schools equipped to handle special problems, while those who attended the island schools were from families that could rarely afford to give money to charity. Suddenly everyone was hugging one another and crying, "Thank you!" The children who understood what the celebration was about clapped their hands and shouted, "Love Banner," and "Save Banner," even though many could not make the connection between the pony and the name.

With the end of the riding program Cindy's duties at the farm lightened perceptibly, but there was still custodial care for the horses and the usual stable work. "You'd have to be crazy to go through this," muttered Faith Bowman the following afternoon, after she had led Ben into a clean stall and he'd promptly urinated.

"Crazy over horses, you mean?" Cindy asked, laughing.

"Yeah, I guess so."

"Well, aren't you? And now you'll have more time to ride Flax."

Each of the girls had a favorite, and Cindy suspected that Faith, a rather homely girl, was drawn to the palomino because of the undeniable beauty of her golden coat.

"That's a plus," Faith agreed. She forked soiled bedding into a wheelbarrow and trundled it outside to the muck rick, then prepared to go home. "Take care," she murmured as she left.

A few minutes later, as Cindy was filling the wheelbarrow with another load of discarded bedding, Tad appeared in the barn door. Cindy was caught by surprise. She hadn't seen him for more than a week, and she had been too absorbed by the progress of the Banner Fund to give him much thought.

"Hi," said Tad. "Just happened to be passing. Thought I'd turn in and see if you were here."

"I'm here." Dirty and tired, Cindy put her fork tines down on the stable floor and leaned on the handle, from which vantage point she eyed Tad speculatively. "Still sore about last Saturday night?"

"I wasn't sore."

"Well, that's good." Cindy chucked another forkful into the wheelbarrow. "I told you I was sorry, and I really am!"

Tad accepted this statement with a quick nod. Then, assaulted by the odor of horse manure, he wrinkled his nose. "For a girl, you sure like dirty work."

"Nobody enjoys mucking out," Cindy replied, "but it's got to be done."

"Don't sound so righteous." Tad leaned against the barn wall and thrust his hands deep into his pockets, watching her, making her feel self-conscious, then belligerent.

"Did you stop by just to criticize me?"

Tad didn't answer, but when the wheelbarrow was filled and Cindy had balanced the fork on top and was about to pick up the handles, he said, "Here, let me." She stepped aside willingly and followed him outside.

"It goes over there," she said, indicating the muck rick. Then, with a sly smile, she trailed along in his wake.

"Do I just dump it?"

"You do not! You fork it up. On top."

The rick was a steep one, several feet above Tad's head. He looked up warily, picked up the fork, and dug out a fair quantity, then stepped back a pace and gave a mighty heave. The forkful landed halfway up the pile and slithered down to the ground.

Cindy burst out laughing while Tad's face turned beet red. "What's so funny?"

"You are!" Cindy retorted, and kept on laughing. When she could finally control herself, she said, "That was mean of me, but you were acting so—so macho."

Tad glared at her.

"There's a trick to it," Cindy said, turning sympathetic. "Here, let me show you." She took the fork out of Tad's hands and, although she was four inches shorter than he, heaved a bunch of the stuff to the top of the pile with little effort.

"How did you do it?" asked Tad grumpily.

"With a flick of the wrist. See, like this. Mrs. Park taught me."

"Let me try again," Tad insisted, and attempted to imitate her quick gesture.

"Good!" Cindy was generous. "You've almost got it."

Suddenly, they were friends again.

As Tad drove her home, he said, "Want to go

skating tomorrow? The rink's open."

Ice skating was not one of Cindy's favorite sports, but she didn't want to turn Tad down again. "What time?"

"How about late afternoon? Then maybe we could go somewhere and grab a hamburger."

"That's fine. I'll be busy in the morning anyway. Want to meet me there?"

Tad shook his head. "I'll pick you up. About four?"

"Four sounds fine."

The next morning Cindy and Caroline accompanied a group of Peter's classmates to Edgartown to supervise the first attempt of the fifth graders to exchange small banners for coins, and only at scattered intervals did she have time to anticipate her date with Tad.

The day was cold and sunny. The children were well wrapped up, and the cans they carried had been primed with handfuls of pennies so they would jingle enticingly. Edgartown was in holiday dress, with store windows decorated and lampposts festooned. Shoppers were out in full force and were inclined to be generous.

A few apparently never read newspapers and didn't know what all the excitement was about, but they contributed anyway. Quarters were abundant, and an occasional dollar bill was crammed into the slots provided. Cindy missed some of the fun because she was stationed out on Edgartown Road in the A&P parking lot, while Caroline supervised the young solicitors from the busy bank corner near the harbor.

"We got some real characters," she told Cindy on the way home. "One little old lady thought she was contributing money to buy a new American flag for the courthouse. There was no use trying to set her straight. She couldn't hear a word I said."

A school bus, commandeered for the morning by a sympathetic driver, dropped the children off at their respective stops and let Peter, Caroline, and Cindy off at Strawberry Hill Road. The girls carried between them a heavy basket filled with cans, while Peter ran on ahead.

"We did good, didn't we?" he called over his shoulder

"Spectacular," Caroline told him. "These cans feel as if they're full of lead."

"I hope not," Cindy murmured.

Her brother turned and waited for the pair to catch up. "Next week maybe the gang who went to Edgartown should go to Oak Bluffs and the week after that to Vineyard Haven. To give them variety, you know." His voice was very serious, and Cindy could tell he had spent some time thinking this proposition through.

"I agree. Also, I think the time on the streets

should be shortened. Some of the smaller kids got too tired."

Peter nodded. "Yeah, but they've got to learn life's not all fun and games, y'know."

Cindy could scarcely suppress a smile because he sounded so much like their father, but she truly appreciated Peter's help. For the first time the age span between them seemed to lessen. They were engaged in doing something important together. However, something else important was coming up. She had to hurry along home, find her skates, and wash her hair. She wanted to look her best this afternoon.

C H A P T E R

HER SKATES! THEY HADN'T been sharpened. "Oh, darn!" Cindy sighed as she ran a thumb over the blunted blades. There was no time to do anything about them now. Tad was due to stop by for her at any minute. She took them to the kitchen and made a few swipes with her mother's whetstone, but it didn't seem to help.

She could confess at once, simply say she had forgotten to have her skates sharpened, as was perfectly natural under the circumstances, but Tad would tease her for being scatterbrained. Besides, he probably wasn't a good skater anyway, being a city-reared boy.

She noticed, however, that the blades of the shoe skates Tad carried into the rink were shiny and razor-keen. Well, maybe they hadn't been used much. Maybe he was just a beginner, Cindy thought hopefully, and lost another chance to explain.

For a Saturday afternoon the rink was uncrowded. "We're lucky," Tad said as they sat on a bench and changed their shoes. "A lot of people are probably off Christmas shopping."

"Hi there!" called a voice from the ice cheerfully, and Cindy looked up to see Caroline skating to a stop in front of them. She was wearing the short pleated skirt that was part of her cheerleader's outfit and a bright red sweater. "You didn't tell me you were coming skating!" she scolded.

"It didn't occur to me," replied Cindy, telling the truth.

Tad, who had finished tying his shoelaces, stood up. "Hello, Caroline. You're looking frisky."

"Whitey, the words you use just slay me. Or did you intend to make me feel like a dog?" Caroline batted her eyelashes as she glanced up at him.

Cindy bent to unlace her shoes, which felt tight and uncomfortable. Had her feet grown so much in a single year? she wondered. "Sorry to keep you waiting," she said, "but I'm going to have to take off these heavy socks."

Unconcerned, Tad tested the ice with a few gliding steps, then came back and caught Caroline's hand. "Take me around once," he suggested. "I'm out of practice."

Cindy looked up as they skated off. She could tell immediately that Tad was no amateur. His long, lean body looked relaxed and graceful. He seemed to skim over the ice as naturally as Caroline, who had always been a superb skater. Halfway around they moved to the center of the rink, where an empty space gave them more room. Tad initiated a few dance steps in time with music coming from a loudspeaker, and Caroline followed him with ease.

Instead of lacing her shoes again, Cindy balled up the offending socks and watched. Out of practice? Tad was good, very good indeed, and Caroline made a responsive partner. They were having fun, as Cindy could plainly see, trying some tricky maneuvers, testing each other. When they returned to the stream of circling skaters and pulled up at the bench, Cindy clapped her hands in admiration. "You're almost as smooth as professionals!"

"That's quite a compliment," Caroline said.

Tad, for his part, asked, "Who are you kidding?"

"I mean it! Of course, Caro's always been super on ice, but where did you learn to skate like that? Not in New York City?"

"I took lessons at Rockefeller Center from the

time I was in second grade, but I never learned to skate as well as my mother. She was really something!" Then, as though this were a confession that had slipped out, Tad moved over and held out a hand. "Come on, Cindy, it's your turn."

"Wait till I finish tying my shoelaces," Cindy murmured, anxious to put off the moment of truth as long as possible. "My skates haven't been sharpened since last winter," she finally admitted, "and my toes are still squashed. It's going to be a disaster."

She was right. She was an indifferent skater at best, and the dull blades bore into the ice instead of sliding over it. She felt like a galumphing rhinoceros as she began breathing heavily, in real fear of falling. Her toes burned and cramped, her shoulders tensed, and she clung to Tad like a lifeline.

"Loosen up," Tad urged.

"I can't."

"What's happened to your self-confidence?"

"I've never had any."

"Ho, ho, ho," intoned Tad with all the heartiness of a street Santa Claus.

Cindy gritted her teeth and essayed a couple of tentative glides, but the tips of her skates dug in and nearly toppled her headforward. "I can't make it," she gasped, and wobbled back to the security of the bench. "Honestly, Tad, my toes are doubled right under. I'm really hurting."

"We could go buy you some new gear right now,"
Tad suggested as he sat down beside her. "It won't
take ten minutes to get to Vineyard Haven."

Cindy shook her head vigorously as she unlaced
her shoes for the third time. "Shoe skates cost too
much. The best I can do is ask for them for
Christmas." And for Christmas, she thought, I have
other priorities.

Caroline was passing the bench again, skating
with another girl, and Cindy beckoned her over. "I
can't even stand up in these three-year-old shoes,"
she said. "When you have a chance, please give Tad
another go."

Tad didn't demur, and Cindy watched the pair
from the sidelines. Other skaters began to watch,
too, clearing a space for them, stopping to admire
their nimble footwork. Caroline's cheeks were
bright pink, and her pleated skirt stood out like a
parasol from her tiny waist as Tad led her in more
and more intricate patterns. Finally she laughed
and threw up her hands, crying, "That's enough!"

Upon leaving her, Tad made a mock bow from the
waist, then skated back to rejoin Cindy. "That was
fun!" he told her. "Your friend's terrific." He sank
down on the bench to catch his breath, then said,
"Let's go, shall we? I'm getting hungry."

Dusk was falling fast. Drivers were switching

their headlights on, and a late plane from Boston was winking from the sky, approaching the nearby airport with a roar that inhibited conversation. Not until Cindy was settled in the pickup did Tad ask, "Where can we get some really *good* hamburgers? Maybe they shouldn't have kept McDonald's off the island."

"McDonald's!" Cindy sniffed with true Vineyard loyalty. "There's a place on the Edgartown harbor that's super, but I'm not sure it's open at this time of year."

"We can try," decided Tad, and turned left from the parking lot while Cindy tucked the offending shoe skates out of sight on the floor.

"The thrift shop for you!" she scolded as if they could hear, then turned to Tad. "I'm sorry about this afternoon. I forgot they were too small, even last year."

Tad grinned. "Forget it. 'Never apologize, never explain,' my mother used to say, and it's a pretty good rule."

This was the second time Tad had mentioned his mother during the past hour, and Cindy took it as a good sign. She couldn't imagine her own reaction to the death of one of her parents. The mere prospect was so unthinkable that she realized Tad had been faced with grief much deeper than any she had ever known. She wished she could lead him to talk more freely about his mother, just as she had confided in him her worries about Banner. But Banner was a horse, not a human being, not a mother, not *her* mother. Reluctantly she realized that she couldn't help Tad. And only through time and courage could he learn to help himself.

Tad drove along a main street nearly empty of shoppers at this time of evening but bright with Christmas lights. Even the harborside seemed festive, although most of the summer boutiques and restaurants were closed. The place on the wharf, however, was open, as Cindy pointed out. The lighthouse beacon swung to touch it in a passing caress, and Tad cried, "Swell! We're in luck."

They found a place by the windows that looked out on the water, even though they were blind and black at night. Soon the days would grow longer again, but in December darkness swooped down on the island as fast as a diving fish hawk. Cindy put her hands to the side of her face and pressed her nose against the pane, peering out, but aside from the steady sweep of the harbor light she couldn't see a thing.

After asking her approval, Tad ordered, and when they were alone, Cindy said, "D'you know, this is the first time we've eaten together."

"Not so. Remember lunch at Gay Head?"

"A picnic doesn't count," Cindy responded.

"Speaking of Gay Head," Tad said as they waited for the food to appear, "I may have a summer job out there."

"Really?" Summer seemed very far away, but even so, Cindy was impressed. After school stopped in the spring, jobs became hard to come by.

"This is sort of unusual," Tad explained. "My history teacher is Mr. Cotton, you know. He's got this friend who is getting his master's at BU and is doing some research on Indians. Anyway, the two of them want to do some digging next summer if they can get permission."

"At Gay Head?"

Tad nodded. "And they may take me on as a helper. Didn't I tell you I've always been sort of keen on archaeology?"

"Not that I remember." Cindy had been so self-absorbed that she was only now becoming aware that she didn't know much about Tad at all.

"Well, anyway, the job wouldn't pay much—just minimum wage—but it might be fun, and it would give me some experience. There are a couple of campsites they want to explore, and I'd be doing the spadework—literally."

"Sounds interesting."

"*I* think so!" Tad's eyes began to sparkle. "I've been reading up on Vineyard history. Did you know this island may have been formed three thousand years ago?"

Cindy knew, as did many other natives, but she shook her head politely.

"Who can tell what may turn up?" Tad asked. "Have you heard about the fellow they found in a Florida peat bog who may be the oldest intact human being ever discovered?"

"Now you're teasing me."

"No, honest. They dug him up just a few years ago, and it made all the papers. Pop kept some articles on the find. You ought to read them."

The waitress put plates of food in front of them, big juicy hamburgers on toasted sesame seed buns. Between bites Tad muttered something about the Wampanoag tribe's being part of the Algonquin nation, but Cindy was too busy eating to pay attention.

"Let's have a hot fudge sundae," Tad proposed when they had finished.

"Such extravagance!" Cindy smiled, but she didn't refuse.

When the dessert arrived, she curled the chocolate sauce around her spoon contemplatively. "Are you thinking seriously about archaeology? As a career, I mean."

Looking thoughtful, Tad gave a slight shrug. "It's too soon to say, but it sure does fascinate me. Whenever I read about student groups flying off to a site in Egypt or Kenya or wherever, I wish I could go along."

Cindy could see the longing in his eyes. "Maybe you will—someday."

"There's college ahead, then graduate school." He spoke as though continuing education were natural and necessary. "Who knows? By then I may change my mind and go in for anthropology. That would be fun, too, except I'm not exactly a whiz at languages."

Cindy gave a sympathetic sigh as Tad put down his dessert spoon and leaned forward to rest his elbows on the table. "One thing's sure. I'll never be a banker or a lawyer or a businessman. The money-making choices are out." He looked at Cindy very seriously and said, "Pop's responsible for my attitude, I guess. I've grown up with a pretty extensive library."

Interested and a little surprised at a side of Tad's personality that had been only hinted at before this evening, Cindy felt out of her depth. "Do most private school boys read a lot?" she asked innocently.

Tad chuckled. "I wondered what you were going to come out with next. You're the most unpredictable girl I've ever known."

Cindy flushed. "And the most naive?"

"In some ways."

"Even Mom despairs of me sometimes. She doesn't think I'm growing up quite on schedule."

Tad chuckled. "Take your time. Or at least go

slow until after Christmas, when I get back from Paris."

"Paris?" Cindy squealed. "Paris, *France*?" Her eyes widened in astonishment.

"Yeah. Pop can't face Christmas on the island, at least not this year. We'll be gone for only a couple of weeks." Tad spoke as casually as if he were saying they intended to spend the holidays in New York.

"Do you have family in Paris?" asked Cindy. Her Christmases had always been decorated by relatives' coming to dinner.

"No, but my father has friends there, and I know a French kid who used to go to Groton. The real reason for going, though, is that Pop is working on a novel with a couple of Paris chapters. He can do some research while he's on the scene."

"That's awesome," Cindy whispered. She was both fascinated and daunted by his news. Since she had seldom been farther away from the island than Boston, even the name of Paris evoked a city that glimmered with picture-book allure. On the way home she kept thinking, Tad's going to Paris, and began to fear that when he returned, he would be a stranger again, unreachable.

"Cindy?"

"Yes?"

"You're very quiet."

"I know."

They were traveling along the shore road that led between Edgartown and Oak Bluffs. The sheltered bicycle path lay on one side, the beach on the other, and above the beach a half-moon hovered in the black sky.

Tad pulled over onto the sandy verge. "Are you too cold to walk a bit?"

"I guess not."

Cindy got down from her side of the cab without waiting for Tad to come around. "Have you ever been to Paris before?" she asked.

"Once."

"I've been to Boston only once." Why she was impelled to talk like an islander, admit her provincialism, Cindy didn't know. She did know, however, that she had to be completely herself with Tad, always. She couldn't hide, as some girls did, behind a make-believe facade, flirting and tossing their hair like birds preening.

Tad took her hand and led her down to tide line, then skipped a few pebbles on the water without uttering a word.

Cindy stood beside him, winding her scarf more tightly around the collar of her coat and drawing on her old woolen gloves. Then she started along the beach toward the dim glow of the Oak Bluffs streetlights, and Tad joined her, reaching for her hand again.

The gloves seemed to surprise him. "Cold?"

"Sure. Aren't you?"

"Want to go back?"

"In a few minutes." The moon offered scarcely enough light to see by, and the tip of her nose felt like ice, yet Cindy felt impelled to keep on walking. After a while Tad tugged the glove off the hand he was holding without speaking. Then he turned her gently and pulled her toward him as his arms went around her. She found herself looking up at his face in the darkness, and instinctively she raised her hand and touched his cool cheek.

Tad's face felt smooth and cold, but his embrace was warm, his arms strong as he leaned down to kiss her upturned lips.

Later, in the car, she became shy again. The headlights illuminated the real world. The walk on the beach was a dream. Disconnected thoughts fluttered through her mind, but the glow persisted. She had liked being held in Tad's arms, his gentle, lingering kiss. Cindy hugged the dream to her heart, like a secret she couldn't share.

CHAPTER
12

BANNER WAS COMING HOME!

Banner was coming home before Christmas, coming back to his own stall in the familiar stable as a convalescent, with a good chance of making a complete recovery by spring.

"It's going to be a long pull," Helen Park warned Cindy. "He'll have to be kept very quiet."

"For how long?"

"All winter, I'm afraid."

The promise that the pony would be back on the island for the holidays spurred the 4-H Club to new efforts. The girls bought a bolt of white sheeting and painted a slogan in red letters: "Make this a Banner Christmas." Then they corralled members of the football team to fasten the sheeting on poles and string it across Main Street in Vineyard Haven. This advertising sign brought in so many contributions that another one was painted for Edgartown.

Meanwhile, the Banner Fund office was receiving mail from all over the country. Letters arrived from as far south as Florida and as far west as Hawaii. Some of them simply expressed personal sympathy for Banner's plight, but many others enclosed money for the pony's medical expenses—as little as thirty-five cents from a child who had broken his piggy bank to pledge it, as much as hundreds of dollars from wealthy off-islanders who had read the AP story and were sufficiently touched to write generous checks. The fund was quickly swelling to nearly a thousand dollars.

Each letter containing a contribution, no matter how small, was answered personally by a volunteer. Sometimes a light burned in the little office until late in the evening. The first snow fell, the *Gazette* ran a follow-up story about the great outpouring of love on Banner's behalf, Cindy continued her work at the farm, and Tad packed a duffel bag for Paris.

On the night before school was scheduled to close for the holidays he showed up at the Fosters' house.

Cindy was wrapping presents at the kitchen table while her mother addressed Christmas cards at the living room desk. "I just came to say good-bye," he explained when Cindy answered the door.

"You must be excited about going to Europe," said Cindy as he followed her out to the kitchen. "Sit down. I'm almost finished."

"I don't have to hold a finger on the string, the way I used to when I was a kid?"

Cindy chuckled and shook her head. "Times have changed."

Tad put a flat package he had been carrying on the table. "This has your name on it," he said. "It's a stocking present, really, but it turned out to be a pretty poor fit."

"Oh, Tad, how nice of you!" Cindy picked up the package wrapped in red and white candy-cane striped paper and stared down at it, trying to hide the confusion that diminished her pleasure. It had crossed her mind that Tad might bring her a present for Christmas, and one day she had even considered buying him a small currency converter for his Paris stay that she had seen in a gift shop, but she was in a hurry, the clerk was occupied, and other concerns had intervened.

Apologetically she finally lifted her eyes to Tad's. "I didn't get you anything, but—"

"I know," Tad interrupted with a sardonic grin. "You haven't had time."

Blushing, Cindy admitted, "I should have made time." Her thoughts roved back to that afternoon in the gift shop. She should have waited for the busy clerk to finish waiting on her other customers. But now it was too late. "Things really have been hectic"—she tried to explain—"what with Banner about to be brought home and all." She caught Tad looking at her in perplexity and blurted out, "I don't know why you put up with me!"

"Sometimes I don't either." Tad spoke with an inflection that might have been either teasing or dead serious. Cindy couldn't tell which.

If only she hadn't been caught wrapping presents. She felt inept, embarrassed, and a glance at the long-limbed boy lounging in a kitchen chair opposite her didn't give Cindy a clue to what to say next.

"When are you leaving?" she asked lamely.

"Tomorrow. We take the night flight from Boston."

The night flight. The very words took wing, carrying Tad out of her life, to a place even more remote than his former off-island world.

"And you come back when?"

"The day after New Year's."

"I hope—I really do hope—you'll have a marvelous time." Cindy spoke to the stranger he might once more become.

"Thanks." Tad stood up. "I told Pop I'd be back

in a flash." He called good night to Mrs. Foster as Cindy went with him to the door. Tentatively, uncertain of her ground, she followed him out to the porch and waited for some sort of farewell gesture. Tad stopped at the top of the steps and turned to look down at her with a sorrowful smile, but he didn't reach out to touch her. "Have a Banner Christmas," he said with a mock salute.

Something had gone wrong, badly wrong, and it was her fault. Cindy realized belatedly that she shouldn't have mentioned the pony. But Banner was very important to her. Couldn't Tad accept that?

Going back into the house, Cindy closed the door softly. I'll make it up to him when he gets home, she promised herself. I'll think of something especially nice.

At the sound of the door shutting, Mrs. Foster turned from the desk and asked, "Something the matter?"

"No." Cindy bit her lip. "Not really."

"Did you get Tad's address in Paris?"

Cindy shook her head. "Why should I?" she asked with a bravado that concealed her sorrow at having hurt his feelings.

"Well, since he brought you a present, I thought you might want to send him a Christmas card."

Cindy took a deep breath. "He'll be home in two

weeks. I can thank him then, Mom."

Mrs. Foster went on addressing envelopes, and Cindy cleared the kitchen table of leftover wrapping paper and ribbon, then went up to her room. She heard her father come in from a conservation meeting just as Peter turned off his radio in the next bedroom. Cindy put Tad's gift out of sight in a bureau drawer. She didn't want to be reminded of it in the morning.

The last day of school before the holidays always seemed frivolous. Teachers were as eager as their pupils to get loose. They made no advance assignments and cracked more predictable jokes than usual. Homemade jellies and jars of brandied or spiced fruit, sent by thoughtful parents of the pupils, appeared on their desks. All this contributed to a festive atmosphere.

The atmosphere was equally festive at Heatherfield Farm, where a welcoming party was planned for Banner. Baskets of apples and carrots, enough for every horse in the stable, had been delivered by some generous Vineyard truck farmers and were waiting in a corner of the barn. Wreaths of island pine, tied with bright red ribbons, decorated windows and the tack room door. Get-well cards and holiday greetings, most of them colored by children using Magic Markers, were tacked to the walls surrounding Banner's stall, and the stall itself had never been cleaner. Cindy and Hope Bowman scrubbed it so thoroughly that it looked antiseptic.

Anticipation grew as everyone waited for the doctors to set the actual date for Banner's return. Laurel came home for the holidays in time to learn that she and Helen Park could drive to New Hampshire to fetch him two days before Christmas. Cindy did not expect to go along, nor was she invited. Instead, she spent the time doing odd jobs around the stable and answering the telephone.

News of the pony's imminent return had traveled throughout the island with the speed of light. Dozens of people called, among them several eager mothers of the handicapped riders. "What time is he expected?" "When can we come see him?" "Joey, or Annabel, or Roy is so excited!"

"Tomorrow afternoon we're having a welcome home party," Cindy told everyone who phoned. "Please come then, between two and four o'clock." Knowing how tired the pony would be from his journey, Mrs. Park had wisely decreed that he should have no visitors on the evening of his arrival.

Cindy was the exception. She would be on hand when Banner set foot on the island once more. With every passing hour her impatience mounted, and as cold penetrated the barn walls and the afternoon light faded, she paced the floor. Stay calm, she told herself, but how could she when she was about to get the Christmas present she most wanted. Banner was coming home!

Bundled in a jacket, Cindy watched the hands of the stable clock turn ever so slowly toward five o'clock. She knew the ferry from Woods Hole must be unloading now, the cars and trucks coming off the gangplank in a steady line. Dominic whinnied and thrust his head toward her over the door of his stall, and Cindy went over to stroke his muzzle and let him lip her hand. "Be a good boy," she told him. "Stay nice and quiet tonight."

Ten minutes more, and she should be able to spot the headlights of Mrs. Park's station wagon as it turned into the farm road. Had the clock stopped? Were the hands still turning? Cindy could scarcely contain herself. She went outside and peered up the hill. Nothing. She grabbed both elbows in her cold hands and tramped up and down, back and forth, beside the barn. A light snow, fine as granulated sugar, misted the sky, and finally, from the distance, a yellow glow was discernible.

Cindy's heart leaped for joy at the sound of a car's motor. She hurried to pull back the barn doors so the trailer could be backed inside, then stood waving both hands above her head in greeting.

"Hi, Cindy!" Laurel jumped to the ground.

"Hi, Laurel. Everything all right?"

"Everything's fine."

Driving with great care, Helen Park edged the trailer through the open door. When she finally cut the motor, it was positioned perfectly at the closest possible distance to Banner's stall.

Stiffly she got out of the driver's seat and walked across the barn to watch the two girls fix the trailer ramp securely. "Long day, Cindy?" she asked.

"Not as long as yours. Lots of people called." She spoke automatically, her eyes on the pony. "Is he all right?"

"He will be," Mrs. Park promised.

Placing his feet warily on the slope, Banner was led out. His right leg was heavily bandaged, and the hoof was still wrapped in a big wad of padding; but Cindy didn't give this more than a cursory glance. If he limped, she didn't notice. When Laurel encouraged him to walk forward, she could only look into his dark eyes.

"When you're buying a horse, never look at his face. You might fall in love." The cautionary words repeated themselves as Cindy reached out to stroke the white heart on Banner's forehead. She made crooning noises in her throat and wished she could hug him when he lifted his head in recognition, but she didn't attempt to touch him again. Just seeing him was enough.

A great many people on Martha's Vineyard

joined Cindy in showing their affection for Banner.
They came to the party the next afternoon along
with some who had never seen him but wanted to
catch a glimpse of the remarkable pony that had
captured the sympathies of contributors from
across the nation.

The Banner Fund had just passed the thousand-
dollar mark and was still growing. To the adults involved it seemed a miracle, but Cindy was hopeful
that they could double the figure. A 4-H leader had
the inspiration to mount a box wrapped in gilt
paper at the barn entrance. There was a big, indica-
tive slit in the top, and it was hoped that in the
course of the afternoon a great deal of small change
and a substantial number of bills would be pushed
through.

Once the party had started, either Cindy or Laurel stayed close to Banner's stall. They had to make
sure the pony wasn't upset by the noise and the
confusion. "No way is he disturbed," Cindy told
Laurel when they were changing posts. "He seems
delighted with all the company."

Some of the children brought apples or carrots,
not knowing that the farm was already well sup-
plied. Adults brought cookies and soda pop for the
visitors. The other horses neighed and stamped in
their stalls, but Banner stood quietly and let all the
guests adore him.

About three o'clock the autistic child who had

missed Banner so grievously that he had burst forth with his name came into the barn with his parents. He immediately dropped his father's hand and walked purposefully toward the pony's stall, bearing a big square of white cardboard.

Cindy was on duty at the time, and she gave him encouragement. "Do you have a present for Banner?"

Herbert nodded, and although he didn't take his eyes off the horse, he held the cardboard up for her inspection. On it he had drawn a lopsided red heart in grease crayon outline. Inside the heart was a bulbous *B* in green, and above the initial were smaller hearts filled in with red and arranged to spell the word *love*.

"That's beautiful! Did you make it all by yourself?"

The boy nodded again, proudly.

"Let's put it on the door of Banner's stall, shall we? I'll go get a hammer and some tacks."

Herbert waited patiently with his parents until Cindy returned, then held the cardboard while she nailed it to the wood. He gestured to his parents and gave them a broad, happy smile that tautened the high cheekbones in his thin face. He took their hands again and brought them close to the pony's stall. Pointing first at the pony's forehead and then at his drawing, he struggled and finally spoke a single word: "Heart."

"That horse has meant everything to him," Herbert's father told Cindy privately when the child and his mother were off touring the stable. "He is trying very hard now, making a real effort to talk."

"I know," said Cindy, "and next spring, when he starts riding again, he'll have new incentives."

Dialogues like this made her feel good, certain that Banner was earning the outpouring of praise and money he was receiving. She thought about Tad in Paris and wished he could have been here today. I wouldn't trade places, though, she thought. I'm glad to be right here, celebrating Christmas in a stable.

Christmas Day itself was almost an anticlimax, although the tree her father had brought from the forest was spangled with familiar ornaments and the weather cooperated by leaving a frosting of snow on the ground. A fire crackled and snapped in the living room fireplace, shooting sparks up the chimney and over the edge of the hearth. "Doggone pitch pine," Mr. Foster complained as he stamped them out.

Opening presents as a plump hen turkey cooked in the oven made Cindy feel more than a little nostalgic. She remembered vividly the years when she had tossed and turned on Christmas Eve, unable to go to sleep from sheer excitement. She remembered, too, the impatience with which she had opened packages, an impatience that even Peter was fast losing. The ceremony was still fun, still a very special family time, but the childish zest she had once felt had disappeared.

Cindy's presents were fewer than usual because the "big one" had been costly. A pair of riding boots—her first—nestled in a froth of blue tissue and smelled of new leather. "You shouldn't have!" she cried at the first glimpse, but her gratitude was boundless.

Peter was equally delighted with a new bike. "Gee, Dad, you must have struck it rich," he commented. His parents laughed, but Cindy intercepted a look exchanged between them and realized that each of these important gifts had entailed a sacrifice.

The one member of the household having every right to be disappointed with his present was Silver. The cat was given a collar with a bell attached to it. "So he will scare the birds," Mr. Foster said.

"Why would he want to scare them?" Peter asked, then looked baffled when everyone laughed.

Cindy opened the package from Tad next to last and found a thin book of selected poems by Robert Frost. On the flyleaf was an inscription in Tad's angular, boyish handwriting: "For my Martha's Vineyard maiden—verses by my favorite New England poet. Merry Christmas! Tad."

How like Tad to give her a book for a present, but what an odd inscription, meaning either a great deal or very little. If only, she thought once again, I had given him something in return!

Riffling through the pages, she came upon some lines she knew, lines that had given the little volume its title:

> The woods are lovely, dark and deep.
> But I have promises to keep,
> And miles to go before I sleep. . . .

As she shut the cover gently, reminded that she had a promise of her own to keep, Peter came and peered over her shoulder. "Who gave you that?" he asked. "It's a funny kind of Christmas present."

Later in the morning, before relatives arrived for dinner, Cindy walked over to the Treats with a gift for Caroline. "Merry Christmas!" she called as she opened the door, and Caroline, still in pajamas and bathrobe, came running downstairs to greet her. "Look!" she cried at once, displaying a wrist encased in a bracelet. "Guess who?"

"Johnny, of course!" said Cindy with a smile.

"Guess again!"

Cindy looked more closely. The bangle attached to the bracelet was a pair of miniature ice skates.

"Wasn't it absolutely darling of Whitey!" Caroline was bubbling. "Just the nicest way of saying he enjoyed skating with me." Caroline jingled the bangle as she drew Cindy toward the stairs. "Come on up and see what else I got."

Stunned, Cindy followed along out of habit. Her mouth felt curiously dry as she inspected the gifts arranged neatly on Caroline's bed and dressing table, trying to make the proper comments but failing miserably. She held out the package she had brought and received one in return but made no attempt to open it. "Uncle Rob and Aunt Mary and the kids are coming for dinner," she said as soon as possible. "I've got to be getting back."

"Cindy Foster, that's a fib, and you know it. It's only eleven o'clock! What's the matter with you?"

"Nothing. Nothing at all." With great effort Cindy kept her voice level.

"Don't try to fool me! You're mad because Whitey gave me this bracelet, and I want to tell you right now I'll never step on your toes, never! About the meanest thing a girl can do is steal somebody's boyfriend."

"Tad isn't my boyfriend!" Cindy shot back.

"You've been dating him."

"Once or twice." Cindy shrugged, trying to appear nonchalant but failing to convince Caroline.

"Anyway, he's yours as long as you want him. When you don't, just let me know."

"He's not *mine*," Cindy said insistently. "Tad's a free agent."

"I don't understand you," Caroline said. "I really don't. You care more about that darned pony than about a really great guy!"

CHAPTER

WHAT COULD SHE DO, Cindy wondered, to set things right with either Tad or Caroline? She felt betrayed by her own tongue, by words spoken in haste, unthinkingly.

Instead of confiding in her mother, asking her advice, as she would have done only a few months before, Cindy decided that this problem was one she would have to work out by herself, yet she tackled it hesitantly.

One evening near the end of the old year she wrote—and rewrote—a polite and noncommittal note to Tad, thanking him for the book of verse and saying she was anxious to hear all about Paris. Maybe, if she acted as if nothing had happened, the memory of his parting words would fade away. She posted the letter in time for it to be in the RD box at the end of the Wainwright's driveway on his return and began to hope that he would phone her.

To handle the situation she had provoked with Caroline was a different matter. Cindy was well aware that she had disavowed any claim to Tad's friendship and she could think of no way to unsay what had been said.

She tried to imagine going to Caroline with an explanation. Look here, she might tell her, I really like Tad; I don't want to hurt him. But would she be hurting Tad if she turned him over to Caro's tender care? Or would she be hurting herself?

Again and again memories of that night on the beach returned to haunt her—the feel of Tad's arms, the way she had instinctively raised her face to his. And other times, too, had been good—sorting books in his father's library, walking for miles at Gay Head.

In the weeks that followed, Cindy felt edgy and restless as she tried to organize her nagging thoughts. Had she misread the tenderness in Tad's kiss? Or had she herself put an end to his friendship with her negligence at Christmastime? Every time the phone rang she raced to answer it, her heart pumping, but Tad's voice never greeted her from the other end of the line.

Nor did he seek her out at school, as he had been accustomed to in the past. The sunless winter days dawned to the sad songs of mourning doves roosting in the trees outside her bedroom window and plodded cheerlessly through the usual long hours in classes. On most afternoons, in the early dusk, she made her way to the farm and tended to Banner. She had learned to change his bandages and even to give him asthma shots when he needed them. He was just as dear as ever but far more subdued now, and his coat, no matter how faithfully Cindy brushed it, didn't acquire its former shine.

"I'm worried about him," Helen Park confessed one day in early February. "He's so terribly lonely."

"But I come almost every day!" Cindy protested.

"You've been great," Helen said at once, "but horses are herd-bound, you know. I think he's pining for the pasture and his four-footed pals."

"When will he be allowed to go outside?" Cindy asked.

"Not until March, the doctors say, when it warms up a bit. And then only on a longe."

Banner looked at them both with sad eyes, as if dismayed by the conversation. "He isn't happy, that's for sure," said Cindy. She began to spend even more time with the pony, trying to cheer him up, but knew in her heart that her effort was useless. His appetite, always ravenous before the accident, fell off, his head drooped, and he endured Cindy's ministrations apathetically.

"Banner won't eat enough. He's getting thin," complained Hope one afternoon when Cindy arrived at the farm later than usual.

"I know." The only time the pony showed any spirit at all was when the horses that had spent the day outside were led in from the wintry fields. They seemed eager to get back inside, and for a short time Banner seemed eager to see them. Then he slipped into lethargy once more and turned his head away from the stall door.

"Banner seems really sick," Cindy told Mrs. Park one afternoon when she had finished putting fresh leg wraps on his knee

"I agree. He isn't responding."

"Can horses become mentally ill?"

"I don't know; but they can certainly go into depression, and that's dangerous. I've phoned the vet, Cindy, and he's coming to look at Banner tomorrow."

Ironically, Dr. Shaw's visit was on Valentine's Day, when there was a renewed abundance of mail addressed to Banner. He received a dried crocus folded into a five-dollar bill, a check for the munificent sum of four hundred dollars, and seventy-eight valentines from island schoolchildren.

"Dr. Shaw is even more worried about Banner than we are," confessed Mrs. Park. "He says if his depression gets much deeper, it could be fatal."

To Cindy the pony's second illness seemed unfair and cruel. After his accident there had been too many things to do in too short a time. Now there was nothing—

"If only we could take him outdoors," she mused. "If only he could move around just a little."

Helen Park nodded. "It's the nature of the animal that he wants to move, but the doctors have warned us that this can be harmful. Still—"

Cindy waited.

"Still, Dr. Shaw said if things get any worse, we'll just have to take the chance."

"Things are bad enough now," said Cindy. She looked at the pony with pity and foreboding. "He's been through a lot, and he was very brave when he had to be; but he's given up. He seems to have lost his will to live."

Mrs. Park squared her shoulders. "We've spent the winter fighting for a miracle," she said. "Banner may have given up, but you and I mustn't! Let's go for broke, Cindy. Let's take him for a short walk!"

Together the girl and the woman, one on either side, led the pony out of the barn through the only door that opened onto level ground. The sun, breaking through heavy clouds, was dropping in the western sky, and the air was damp and fresh. Banner raised his head a few inches and took some long breaths, then craned his neck and looked wistfully down toward the pastures.

"Not today, boy," Mrs. Park said. "One step at a time."

Slowly and patiently the pair led the pony back and forth on the trampled turf. He favored his injured knee but seemed to enjoy the exercise, and when they returned him to his stall, he took a long drink of water and nibbled at his fodder. Cindy was encouraged for the first time in weeks.

"I don't think it has hurt him," she said to Mrs. Park.

"On the contrary. Often doctors can be overly cautious when they're not on the scene. But it's going to take time."

A lot of time! Cindy increased the hours she spent at the farm so that she could exercise Banner daily. Once more he resumed his former habit of pricking his ears on her arrival, and he behaved in a mannerly fashion when she took him out for his walk.

Gradually, very gradually she increased the distance he traveled, and by the end of the month he managed to negotiate the slope that led to the farm road. From then on the walks became more interesting. Cindy led him past fenced fields that would be high with corn or sprawling with melon vines next summer. Out in the open, away from the closeness of walls, he appeared to walk with a firmer tread.

In all this time Cindy had seen Tad only casually. Occasionally they passed in the school corridors, but she no longer dashed hopefully to the telephone when it rang at home. Since he had come home, Tad hadn't phoned, nor had he asked her out again. Cindy almost persuaded herself she was too busy to care. Nevertheless, she missed him.

Tad was playing basketball this semester, according to occasional reports that drifted her way. Since she had no time to watch practice or go to games, she didn't even learn whether he played on the varsity.

Although she still sat with Caroline on the morning bus, Cindy no longer felt at ease with her. Once or twice during long weeks when she worked at the farm harder than she had ever worked in her life, she mentioned Banner's condition. Each time Caroline made clucking sounds of commiseration but didn't seem truly interested.

On the first Saturday evening in March, after a bleak day of wind and freezing rain that kept the pony confined to his stall, Cindy was at home with her family. "Hey, listen to this!" exclaimed Peter, who was lying on his stomach on the living room floor turning the pages of the *Gazette*. "The skating rink's closing for the season, and they're having a farewell exhibition tonight. Let's go, okay?" He looked directly at Cindy.

"Oh, Peter, I don't know—" said Cindy.

Her father interrupted. "Let's all go," he suggested surprisingly. "Do us good to get out."

"In this weather?" his wife protested weakly.

"Sure. It's only a hop, skip, and jump. I'll drive carefully."

Peter was delighted, and Cindy went along from sheer inertia.

Crowded into a makeshift grandstand at one end of the rink were nearly a hundred islanders, many of them friends. Too far away for conversation, the Treats waved to the Fosters, and the Fosters waved back.

Cindy, noticing that Caroline wasn't with her parents, wondered if she had a date with Johnny. Or perhaps with Tad? The unwelcome thought was discarded almost as fast as it occurred to her. Unless Caroline was skating in the exhibition, the Treats were unlikely to be here. Photocopied programs had run out before the Fosters arrived, so Cindy had no means of checking.

Soon the lights dimmed, a chorus line of young girls swung out to open the show, and appropriate music followed their movements. The girls didn't quite keep pace. They were cautious and a little slow, amateurs doing their best to look professional and terrified of taking a tumble. Cindy was drawn to them by their need to excel—and by their inadequacy. She applauded longer than necessary when they left the ice, then sat through a less-than-funny comedy routine performed by young men dressed as clowns. A group of more experienced skaters wearing tutus followed and made a valiant attempt at a ballet corps routine from *Swan Lake*.

Cindy wriggled uncomfortably. The board seats were hard, and the air was becoming stuffy. Perhaps Caroline wouldn't appear after all. Then a spotlight focused on the center of the rink, the canned music shifted to a Viennese waltz, and out skated a princess with strawberry blond hair wearing a black chiffon waltz-length costume that enhanced every line of her slender figure.

"Hey, that's Caroline!" Peter piped.

"Sh."

"She's lovely," whispered Cindy's mother.

Cindy nodded. "She looks so grown-up."

Caroline made a few graceful passes across the ice, then turned her head away from the audience as though she were looking for someone. On cue, a male skater in a tuxedo moved out on the ice to join her. Caroline held out a hand, and he grasped it lightly. Together they whirled in an airy waltz, dipping, bending, parting, returning. Caroline, looking deceptively fragile, smiled up at Tad Wainwright's face, alight with approval. Cindy stifled a gasp.

She kept her eyes straight ahead, watching every movement, while her stomach muscles clenched and her teeth locked tensely. Life had not prepared her for the way she felt about seeing Tad with Caroline. She couldn't help admiring the performance. It was an elegant finale to a tiresome evening, but while Cindy watched Tad match Caroline's fluid grace with smooth, often intricate dance steps, she felt both physically ill and furious. Like a slap in the face, realization came. She was wildly, incredibly jealous!

For such a reaction she scolded herself bitterly. Whatever her relationship to Tad had been, it was over. The past could not be recalled. Of course he hadn't been interested in her in a special way, no matter what his kiss or the inscription in his gift book had implied.

Of course she must conceal her feelings. When applause swept the stands, Cindy slapped her hands together and managed a spurious smile. "They're marvelous, aren't they?" she said to her mother, who was sitting next to her.

"They're very good indeed," Mrs. Foster replied. "Where did they ever learn to skate together like that?"

"Right here at the rink," said Cindy.

"Wait till I see Ed Treat! His little girl's a natural," her father leaned across Peter to say. "So's that boy she was skating with."

"That's Tad, Daddy. You know him. He used to come to see Cindy."

Used to. The words bit into Cindy's consciousness like the assault of a snarling dog. She wanted to take Peter's shoulders and shake him until his teeth rattled, but she had to keep up a good front. She had to sit calmly through the ensemble lineup and watch Tad and Caroline come forward for a sweeping bow. Tad's hair looked white in the floodlights, but his face looked very smooth and young. And he appeared perfectly natural and happy. Obviously he was having a great time.

Peter was as impressed as if Tad were a celebrity. "Hey, where d'you suppose he got that nifty suit?" he asked Cindy on the way out to the car.

"Probably borrowed his father's dinner jacket," Cindy replied stiffly. "They're about the same height."

"Boy, he looks really good all dressed up."

His father laughed. "How about Caroline?"

With a shrug Peter said, "She was all right." His praise, however, was tinged with contempt, because Caroline was a girl.

In the back seat of the car, riding home, he began to bait Cindy, who was sitting as far away from him as possible. "Dummy," he said, "you sure let a good one get away."

Wishing she could kick her brother in the shins, Cindy manufactured a yawn. "Mind your own business," she advised.

Once back at the house, Cindy fled. Refusing an offer of hot chocolate, she went up to her room, shut the door, and locked it. Then, without undressing, she flung herself facedown across the bed.

CHAPTER
14

JEALOUSY, CINDY DISCOVERED in the days that followed, was an emotion so ugly and pervading that she couldn't conquer it. Appearing like a goblin in the troubled dark before dawn, it would prick her awake and taunt her! Yah, yah, yah! Aren't you sorry you didn't listen to your mother?

Cindy tossed and turned and secretly hated everyone. Hiding behind her involvement with Banner, she began riding her bicycle to school so that she wouldn't have to sit with Caroline on the bus. She had congratulated her, of course, on her performance—"You've come a long way, baby! Seriously, you should think of taking special lessons and going professional someday."

(And move away from Martha's Vineyard. Far away!)

To Tad she said sweetly, "You and Caro saved the evening. You skate beautifully together!" She tried desperately to hide her hurt and make her smile appear genuine.

"Gee, thanks," said Tad, looking pleased. "I didn't know you were there."

He hadn't meant to be cutting. Sarcasm wasn't Tad's style. However, the words rankled, smothering any hope that he might still like her, that he might remember with some small joy that night before Christmas when they had kissed on the wintry beach. She hurried away and tried to still her racing blood. All right, she told herself, the gong has been struck, the crisis is over. As one cliché followed another in her thoughts, she determined—no matter what!—to get on with her life.

As the weeks of March crept by and angry storms alternated with misty sunshine, Cindy discovered that even the daggers of jealousy dulled with time. She walked Banner down the hill and through the woodland bridle paths, making sure that no fallen branch lay in his way, that his pace was slow and steady. Wildflowers, sheltered by damp oak leaves, appeared along the sandy trails. Arbutus peeked through the winter's mulch. Snowdrops opened their bell-shaped blossoms. Banner stepped carefully, avoiding them. Could he possibly know how precious they were?

Cindy chided herself for such a ridiculous fancy, but she found the hours spent with the pony soothing and the hints of spring a tonic for her soul. By the first of April the handicapped riders would return for their weekly classes, and she wanted Banner and the season to be ready for them.

Helen Park agreed that the pony's spirits had improved greatly. His interest in life was returning. His eyes were brighter, his coat increasingly glossy. New X rays were taken of the injured knee and sent to the Equine Center, where a surgeon reported that if he hadn't been on the operating team, he wouldn't have known there had been a fracture.

"So that means the kids can ride him again?" asked Cindy.

"The smaller ones," replied Mrs. Park cautiously. "We don't want to put much weight on his back. He's not ready for it."

The day of the first class was clear and windless, although it was unseasonably cold. Several of the children had met Banner during the autumn term, and they made a great fuss over him; but the newcomers had to be introduced to him, as well as to Dominic and the other horses that would be working with them in the ring. On this day much of the time was spent in the stable, because the handicapped children were almost all sensitive to cold, which could make them edgy and difficult.

Banner seemed to enjoy the commotion in the barn. The shouts and occasional screams of the children didn't annoy him. He allowed himself to be stroked and patted and looked at them with pleasure in his eyes. "I think he's anxious to return to work," Cindy said to the volunteers.

"Where's the heart? The heart on his forehead?" Roy called out. Hyperactive as usual, he was trying to climb the wooden door to Banner's stall.

"Right here." Cindy brushed away the lock of hair that fell between his ears, hiding the white patch. "Before next week I'll cut his bangs."

Leaning to within a few inches of the pony's face, Roy laughed uproariously, but Banner didn't flinch. His manner remained mild and interested all afternoon. Cindy was very proud of him.

With the perversity of early April the weather turned warm a few days later. In Edgartown one late afternoon Cindy was coming out of the drugstore when she noticed the Wainwrights' red pickup parked in front. Tad was nowhere to be seen, but Mr. Wainwright was about to get into the driver's seat when he recognized Cindy. He came around the hood and said, "Nice to see you!" with genuine warmth, then astonished her by adding, "You've lost some weight. It's very becoming."

Flushing in confusion, Cindy admitted, "I've been working hard."

Glancing at the sky, Mr. Wainwright said, "Isn't this a lovely day! A perfect afternoon for the first ice cream cone of the season, but I can't parade down the street eating one all by myself. Let me buy you one, too?"

The invitation was irresistible, and so—come to think of it—was Tad's father. Ten minutes later Cindy sat beside him on a bench outside the ice cream store licking away at the sides of the cone and looking out over the harbor toward Chappaquiddick. "The water looks almost blue today," she said inconsequentially. "I miss all the boats, though."

Mr. Wainwright took a big bite out of his coffee ice cream, said, "Mm," then turned to Cindy. "I've missed *you.*"

Did he expect an answer? What was there to say? Cindy kept on swiping her tongue around the mound of ice cream and stared at the yacht club dock. As the silence lengthened, she was rescued by a direct question. "How's Banner doing these days?"

"Wonderfully!" Cindy replied, not surprised that Tad's father knew the pony's name. He had become an island celebrity over the winter. The Banner Fund had reached twenty-five hundred dollars and was still growing.

"Can you ride him again?"

Cindy shook her head. "Not yet. It's going to be a long convalescence. He's working with the handicapped kids, though."

"Tell me, do these children actually learn to ride?"

"Only a few. Most of them have poor muscle tone, but we help them improve their balance and coordination." Relieved that the conversation had shifted away from the personal, Cindy warmed to the subject she knew best. "They love the smell, the warmth, and the motion of horses. You'd be surprised—"

At intervals, while finishing their cones, Mr. Wainwright kept asking questions and Cindy kept answering. Her eyes bright with enthusiasm, she explained how proud and happy the children felt if they managed to learn, after special exercises and great effort, to sit properly on a saddle and hold the reins.

"Idealism is alive and well and living on Martha's Vineyard," Mr. Wainwright murmured when Cindy finally stopped talking.

"Are you teasing me?"

"No. I'm serious, Cindy. Idealism is an important part of American life. What you're doing at Heatherfield Farm—brightening things up for these kids—isn't just a pat on the head, you know. It's good work, in a good cause. It's also a form of idealism."

"Then you approve?"

"Most certainly. I wish you'd ask Tad to stop by someday and see what's going on."

Cindy frowned, put off by the very thought. "Oh, I couldn't do that!"

"Why not?"

This was an unanswerable question. She simply shook her head.

Mr. Wainwright sighed, straightened his knees, and stretched his legs, looking down at his boots. "Tad likes you, Cindy."

"Not anymore."

As if she hadn't spoken, he said, "He may even be a little bit in love with you, although he'd never admit it. He's terribly jealous."

"Tad? Don't be silly!" Cindy was shocked into saying. "Jealous of whom?"

"Of Banner, of course."

"That's impossible!" Cindy objected, but was this so unlikely as it seemed? She remembered Tad's last remark before his trip to Paris: "Have a Banner Christmas." "Banner's a horse."

"Precisely." Mr. Wainwright chuckled. "Let's

make an educated guess. Tad's feelings are hurt. Why? Because you're horse crazy, he thinks. You won't give him any time."

"He hasn't exactly sought me out," Cindy protested sorrowfully.

"Aha! So we've come full circle. Just to please me, ask Tad to look in on a riding class. *Show* him what you've accomplished. Take my word for it, Cindy, although he's not interested in horses, he's still interested in you."

Clasping her hands, Cindy pondered the proposition. "What if you're wrong?" In her mind's eye she could see Tad dancing with Caroline on the ice.

Mr. Wainwright shrugged. "What would you lose? Think it over." He got up from the bench and held out his hand to Cindy in a gesture so like Tad's that it made her heart flutter.

"This is the strangest conversation I've ever had with a grown-up," Cindy said as they walked up Main Street together.

Mr. Wainwright laughed. "It was pretty strange for me, too."

"Anyway, thanks for the ice cream cone."

"And, my young friend, thanks for your time!"

In spite of the difference in their ages, Cindy felt curiously at ease with Mr. Wainwright. His remarks sometimes perplexed her, but she could talk to him naturally, as she no longer seemed to be able to talk to her parents. And she gave his suggestion a great deal of thought. What did she have to lose, after all, if she invited Tad to look in on a riding class? Her self-esteem?

Yes, Cindy had to admit, that was it. Her self-esteem was at risk, and the thought of a turndown was daunting; but in order to prove herself to Mr. Wainwright—and perhaps prove him wrong!—she gathered her courage.

When the time came, courage failed her, but she gathered it again—and again. Finally she accosted Tad on the way to the lunchroom and asked, in a manner she hoped sounded nonchalant, "Tennis started yet?"

"Next week."

His eyes were wary, his mouth unsmiling, Cindy noted, and almost lost her nerve. Then she gathered herself together for a final time. "I was wondering—" Breaking off, she swallowed hard, then continued in a rush. "Maybe you'd like to come by the farm tomorrow afternoon and watch the horses work out with the handicapped kids."

"Tomorrow?" Tad sounded dubious.

"They come every Thursday at three," said Cindy, clutching at a straw to avoid an outright refusal.

Tad hesitated. "Well, maybe. If I have time."

Time. The word Cindy had so sadly overused returned to taunt her. However, she forced a smile and urged, "Please try." Then, pretending to be in a hurry, she scurried off without a backward glance. Tad won't come, she told herself. I know it!

Yet she hoped. That night she washed her hair and after her shower stood before the bathroom mirror, inspecting her body. She *was* thinner, and her figure seemed to be improving. In pajamas she sat propped up in bed and manicured her nails, sorry that stable work had broken two down to the quick. In the morning she selected a sweater that was almost new and a shirt not yet faded from washing.

"You look especially nice," her mother told her at breakfast. "Anything going on?"

"The kids come riding every Thursday, remember?" This was a poor excuse for the care she had taken, but Cindy couldn't possibly admit that she had primped for Tad Wainwright.

The afternoon was gray, the horses restless when she arrived at the stable. Mrs. Park was on hand, along with a couple of 4-H counselors, and it was decided to take three horses—Dominic, Big Ben, and Banner—down to the lower field.

Several mothers and a couple of teachers arrived along with the bus and walked down the hill to look on. There was no sign of Tad, or of any other boy for that matter. As usual, this was a strictly female operation.

In spite of a searing disappointment, Cindy was

able to devote her complete attention to the children. There were those who responded to the challenge of riding horseback and those who reneged. There were tempers to be dealt with and fear to be assuaged.

"Banner! I want the Black Stallion!" shouted Roy at the beginning of class.

"We take turns on the pony," Cindy told him. "He's not quite well yet." When the little boy began to pout and stamp his feet, she leaned down and whispered, "Maybe next week."

A thin child in leg braces, new to the program, hoisted himself to the mounting block, determined to get up on Banner's back unassisted. "Let Randy try," said one of the volunteers to Cindy, who nodded and brought the pony into position. Banner was still too stiff to lower his back helpfully, as he had taught himself to do at the fall session, but he stood very still while Cindy stroked his forelock and the boy struggled valiantly.

In the end Randy couldn't make it. He was disappointed but not defeated. "Can I try again next time?" he asked when he was helped into the saddle.

Cindy had become so engrossed that she had eyes and ears only for Randy and her beloved Banner. She didn't see Tad join the spectators and stand behind a couple of tall women wearing stout woolen coats. The class was almost over when she became aware of his presence; then her heart turned over with a jolt of pleasure. She caught his eye and waved.

Tad waved in return and came over to the fence as the group dispersed. The other horses had to be exercised by the 4-H girls as a reward for their patience with the children, but Banner still had to be walked rather than ridden. "I usually take him back through the woods," Cindy told Tad when she led the pony through the gate. "Want to come along?"

"Sure." Hands stuffed into his jacket pockets and shivering slightly in the brisk northeast wind, Tad strolled at Cindy's side. To be chilly belied the season, because spring had come to the Vineyard. A tractor was crawling along in a nearby field, turning the decayed corn stubble and winter-beaten grass to expose rich, damp earth. This time of plowing was a new beginning, or so Cindy hoped.

Once in a while Tad turned and looked back at Banner. " 'You know how it is with an April day/ When the sun is out and the wind is still . . .' " he murmured.

Cindy laughed, recognizing the quotation. "Except that it's darned cold!" She continued softly, " 'You're one month on in the middle of May./ But if you so much as dare to speak'—"

Tad stopped her. "So you've read the book."

Cindy nodded. "And loved it."

Turning to look back at Banner again, Tad dared not only to speak but to change the subject abruptly. "I'm impressed."

"I hoped you would be. He's a remarkable pony!"

"I'm impressed by you, Cindy, and the care you take with those children. But what's remarkable is how forcefully the feeling you and Banner have for each other comes through." Tad sounded shaken. "I never realized—"

"I've always loved Banner. I always will." Cindy spoke openly, proud of their mutual affection. "He still needs me, Tad, but he isn't mine. He belongs to a wonderful girl, Laurel Proctor. She loves him, too."

With a dry chuckle indicating an abrupt change of mood, Tad muttered, "The classic triangle. Aren't you jealous?"

Newfound wisdom prompted Cindy to reply, "You can't be jealous of a horse."

Tad lifted his head and spoke to the air, to the trees that arched over the path. "Oh, can't you!"

"Not the way you can be jealous of a person."

"Speaking from experience?"

Cindy nodded. Here was a chance to clear the air. She could admit to her feelings now or perhaps never. She took a long breath and said, "When I saw you and Caro dancing together on skates, I wanted to die."

There, it was out! The unspeakable had been spoken. The world could start moving again, and did. As they entered the woods, a squirrel scampered up the trunk of a nearby tree. A few needles drifted down, and a pinecone fell. Tad stopped walking, stood thinking. "Why?" he asked finally. "What bugged you? I thought you said we looked pretty good."

Tad had misunderstood! Recovering from shock, Cindy said, "You looked dreamy. As if you were made for each other."

"Me and Caroline? No way!"

"Oh, come on, Tad!" Cindy could laugh now. "I saw you!"

"So we're great onstage. That doesn't mean a thing. There are dozens of skating partners—real pros—who really mesh on ice but who can't stand each other in real life."

Cindy gave a skeptical snort.

"You'd better believe me! Caroline's got talent, but she's not a girl I'd want to date. I've missed you, Cindy."

As if she had been offered paradise on a silver platter, Cindy looked up into his eyes. "I've missed you, too."

CHAPTER

15

THINKING IT OVER, CINDY couldn't recall that much actually had been said in the conversation, but she felt contented and at peace. Her world was back in order.

And Tad began phoning again, at odd hours. At first he wanted only to talk, and Cindy wanted only to hear his voice, to keep him talking. Easing gradually back into a friendly relationship seemed natural and right, for neither of them was in a hurry. If Cindy couldn't go out when Tad asked her, she explained frankly, and he understood, no longer believing she was hiding behind a horse. He even came to the farm and helped Cindy with stable work on afternoons when he wasn't playing tennis.

Tad played a lot of tennis, whenever the showery April weather permitted. He played singles with junior and senior boys and was a shoo-in on the high school tennis team. He also played doubles as Caroline's partner occasionally and told Cindy about it.

"That girl's got coordination built in."

Cindy agreed. "She could do everything better than I could, even when we were little." If the merest trace of envy remained, she determined to expunge it by repeating Tad's praise to Caroline. "He really admires you."

"Gee, thanks," said Caroline, then asked with a hopeful smile, "You're not mad at me anymore?"

Cindy shook her head. "I was wrong about you two," she admitted, and went off feeling the better for the apology.

As the weather warmed, Banner limbered up. Cindy began riding him carefully, taking him from a walk into a trot but, of course, not attempting a canter or a gallop. The pony's spirits rose with the increasing exercise. He responded kindly to the attentions of the handicapped children, but his times with Cindy were the high points of his days.

She took him along a trail beside the lagoon, where Canada geese and mute swans sometimes appeared from inland ponds. She walked him up and down hills to strengthen his muscles. Dreamily she was aware of the return of the island songbirds: scarlet tanagers, warblers, an occasional oriole.

Springtime rites on the Vineyard didn't change much. Farmers finished plowing their fields and looked at the new leaves on oak trees to determine the time for planting corn. Little girls skipped rope in village schoolyards just as they had in Cindy's grandmother's day. Cindy and Caroline, in their season, had been expert at Double Dutch.

Cindy started to ride the morning bus again, and Caroline welcomed her back with whispered confidences. "Some of the kids are coming to my house Saturday night. Mom and Dad have promised to stay out of the way. Why don't you and Whitey come over?"

In a way Cindy was pleased, because the invitation implied acceptance, but in another way she was wary. She had no interest in sitting with other couples in a darkened living room, listening to tapes or watching rented movies. Yet she had no excuse to offer, not even a lame one. "Can I let you know?" she asked.

"Sure."

Cindy didn't even consult Tad, nor did she attempt to explain that they didn't have dates like Caroline and Johnny's. Mostly they went out together in the daytime. So she just said, "Sorry, Tad and I have other plans," and let it go at that.

Actually she and Tad met around noon on Saturday, as they did most weekends when they had taken to roaming the island together. They went off on various adventures, exploring windy Katama Beach where Atlantic combers crashed noisily on the sand, discovered a hidden pond near West Tisbury filled with hundreds of wild swans, watched the ospreys at Felix Neck build untidy nests atop tall poles.

That day they went rock collecting on the head at Vineyard Sound near Lake Tashmoo and at dusk ended up at Tad's house, where Cindy helped cook dinner. Mr. Wainwright went off to a cocktail party, so that night they ate alone, then sat out on the farmhouse steps and looked down over the meadow.

"Nice day, wasn't it?"

"Lovely," said Cindy. "By the way, Caroline asked us to a party tonight at her house."

"And you said we couldn't come?" Tad yawned and stretched. "Good. I don't go for group smooching."

Cindy laughed. "It's not necessarily—"

"Oh, yes, it is!" Leaning back on his elbows, Tad stared down toward the duck pond, now almost invisible. "One thing I like about the island, there isn't the hassle to do things and be things before you're ready. You can grow up at your own speed, the way you're doing."

"At a slow crawl."

"That's all right, if it suits you." Tad took a long breath of the night air and said meditatively, "Spring is really great this year!"

By the middle of May windows were thrown open in the high school classrooms, and the fragrant air routed the stale, chalky smell of winter. Cindy felt pleasantly lethargic one moment and bursting with energy the next. Like everyone else, she couldn't wait for school to be over. Summer plans were being made. Boys were vying for jobs at ferry docks, supermarkets, and gas stations. Girls were contacting summer people who might need baby-sitters or household helpers. Tad phoned one evening with great news. "Hey, that Gay Head job I told you about is all set! I'll have some spending money."

"Don't you always?"

"Not that much. Pop can be kind of tightfisted."

"I don't believe it. Your father's a swell guy!"

"Lay off. He's too old for you, Cindy."

"Honestly, I don't think you appreciate him!"

"Pop's okay," Tad admitted, "except when he's writing a book. Then I can't even talk to him."

"Join the club," suggested Cindy. "It's not your father that's the problem. It's your age, Tad." She chuckled sagely. "Why don't you start growing up, like me?"

By the first of June arrangements were under way for the annual Fourth of July parade, which traditionally took place in Edgartown at five o'clock in the afternoon. Cindy was at the farm when Helen Park got a phone call from one of the organizers. "Banner is invited to join the line of march as a featured attraction," she told Cindy. "I'm not at all surprised."

Nor was Cindy, although she turned thoughtful. "He can't walk all the way to Edgartown!"

"Of course not. But if we take him to the school grounds in the trailer, I think he can manage the swing through the village streets."

"Will Laurel ride him?"

"I suppose so. That's up to her."

Of course Laurel would ride him. Cindy knew the answer even as she asked the question. By July her school would have closed for the summer—or did girls studying nursing have to go to classes year-round?

That slender hope was dashed when Laurel showed up during the week of final exams at Vineyard High. Not only was she eager to ride in the parade, she was also ready to take over Banner's daily exercise sessions. "So you can spend more time studying," she said to Cindy.

Cindy didn't want to study. She wanted to go with Banner through the green June woods, where jack-in-the-pulpits were nodding their heads in moist places and the pink ladyslippers that had bloomed so bravely in May still had some color. Yet in a way she was grateful, because cramming for exams might improve her grades, which had been slipping ever since the pony's accident.

Tad started his summer job the day after school let out. "I'll have my first week's pay by the Fourth," he said. "Let's celebrate! We'll catch the parade, then go out for a lobster dinner, and wind up watching the fireworks at Oak Bluffs."

"Sounds wonderful!" Cindy stifled the slight wistfulness she felt when the parade was mentioned. If she couldn't ride Banner, at least she could make sure he looked his very best, and she spent hours at the farm helping Laurel groom him.

Together the two girls soaped his mane and tail, combed them out, and braided yarn into them. They took electric razors to his nostrils and hooves while he stood calmly listening to the buzzing that would have spooked a nervous horse like Flax. They brushed his coat until it shone like velvet.

Meanwhile, the Vineyard geared up for a gala weekend. To handle the crowds, five extra round trips were added to the ferry schedule. Inns had been booked to capacity weeks in advance, and yacht club marinas were filled with visiting sail-boats, yachts, and motor cruisers.

The morning of the Fourth was hot and steamy. Everybody headed for the beach, including the Fosters, who always went early and came home for lunch. By eleven o'clock the Atlantic coast was crowded. People laden with all sorts of beach paraphernalia arrived and set up housekeeping. The waves off Katama were foamy and great for riding, although the water was still cold, really just bearable. Peter stayed in too long and returned to his parents with chattering teeth and violet lips. "Same as last year," his father said while his mother rubbed him down with a towel.

Cindy went for a dip but stayed close to her parents for most of the morning because it was—and always had been—a family holiday. This year she would be breaking tradition by going off with Tad later, and she wanted to let them know she still treasured their good times together.

Tad was late in picking her up in the afternoon. "You wouldn't believe the traffic on the road to Edgartown," he complained. "Up-island it's dead. Does everybody always go to the parade?"

"Always," Cindy told him. "After three-thirty you can forget about driving into town. We'll have to park on the outskirts."

She had hoped to stop by the school grounds to

see Banner before parade time, but it was far too late. Instead, she and Tad joined the throng walking down Main Street past Pease's Point Way, where American flags fluttered from white clapboard houses built centuries ago. A band was warming up in the distance, but the sound was muffled by laughter and talk all around them.

There were children holding tiny flags in one hand and ice cream cones in the other, barefoot girls in shorts and halters, babies in strollers, boys in fringed cutoff jeans, people on canes or in wheelchairs, young parents in conversation with their offspring or friends. Cindy smiled at some, spoke to others, and introduced Tad to a special few. Then a rumble of drums alerted the waiting crowd, and children ran to find places to sit on the curbs while teenagers and adults gathered behind them.

"Gee, they're polite!" whispered Tad to Cindy as he saw taller people step back and urge shorter ones forward. "When I think of Macy's Thanksgiving parade on Broadway, it makes me feel as if I'd stepped back in time."

Cindy smiled. "People say we're still living in the nineteenth century, but of course that's not true. We even have cable TV. We keep in touch." She spoke teasingly but with an islander's unconscious pride.

The band music swelled, and the first marchers appeared. World War II and Korean War veterans were followed by soldiers who had fought in Vietnam. Next came open convertibles filled with town leaders, and then all the Edgartown police who could be spared from duty stepping to a march played by the Bay State Band.

"This is the dull part," Cindy whispered to Tad. "It gets better."

A dozen local firemen appeared, pulling the department's prize antique engine, an 1855 Button Tub pumper with white wooden wheels, iron rails, and a brass bell. Everybody cheered, and cheered again when an out-of-season Santa Claus came by on a shiny new fire truck. "Whaddaya want this year?" he shouted to the curb sitters, but any responses were lost in the general hubbub.

"I can hardly wait!" Cindy breathed. She craned her neck and peered down the street in search of Banner, but all she could see was a group of gymnasts tumbling on the macadam, followed by a string of old cars. Floats, including one carrying people wearing Indian headdresses, appeared.

"What's that about?" Tad asked Cindy.

"I'll tell you later." Right now she was trying to read the words on a banner carried by three teenagers: "We shall require a substantially new way of thinking if humankind is to survive."

"Wow! Albert Einstein?" asked Tad. "That's pretty heavy stuff."

Where was Banner? Cindy shifted restlessly and

turned to scan the line of march again. Then, far in the distance she saw him, a single horse pacing along slowly with a girl in riding clothes on his back.

"He's coming!" Cindy slipped her arm through Tad's.

Appropriately, it seemed to her, the valiant pony was preceded by the Glengary Highland Pipe Band, the members dressed in tartan kilts, knee socks with tassels, and sporrans with fringes. On cue from the drum major they raised their bagpipes, and the music of Scotland filled the air. For more than twenty years they had marched in the Edgartown parade, and they always drew the loudest applause.

Along with everyone around her, Cindy began to clap, and the clapping went on as the band was followed by a busload of handicapped children. A legend on the side of the bus read BANNER RETURNS, and a number of children were leaning out the windows and pointing at their favorite horse with a red-haired girl in his saddle.

"Why the big fuss?" asked an off-islander standing next to Tad.

"If you lived here, you wouldn't have to ask. That's the most famous horse in the whole state, maybe in the whole world!" piped up a grammar school child at the man's elbow. "His name is Banner, and we love him."

Tears came to Cindy's eyes. She couldn't hold them back. Tad squeezed her arm and hugged her close to his side. "He walks without any limp at all!"

Cindy nodded through her tears. "He's beautiful, isn't he?"

"Beautiful," Tad agreed, although he was looking at Cindy instead of at the pony.

"So is Laurel. She looks so proud!"

"She should be. Proud of *you*."

Cindy shook her head. "It took a lot of people to bring Banner back, Tad. But if he hadn't been so brave—and so intelligent—he'd never have made it. This is Banner's day."

Looking down at her, Tad wondered aloud, "Do you wish you were riding him?"

Cindy didn't have to search for an answer. "I'd rather be here with you."

Applause swelled again as horse and rider moved past. Laurel nodded and smiled and stroked Banner's neck in praise, and the islanders cheered and waved. Those who knew were delighted that the Banner Fund had finally reached its goal. Here was living proof that the effort had been worthwhile, a healthy pony with a white heart on his forehead, beloved by island children.

Cindy brushed the back of her hands across her eyes. "I don't know why I'm crying. Yes, I do. Because I'm really, truly happy."

Later—much later—smelling faintly of lobster and lemon juice, Cindy and Tad spread a blanket on a spare rectangle of grass near the Ocean Park gazebo. In the lighted bandstand more than forty musicians were warming up, and in a vast semicircle the Victorian houses of Oak Bluffs looked down on the greensward. People were everywhere, on porches and balconies, in the park, on the street fronting the sound.

Fog rolled in with early evening, a natural result of the humid day, but even so, the Firemen's Civic Association was bound to draw several thousand people to the annual display.

"Will the fireworks be fuzzy?" Tad wondered.

"Even if they are, they'll be nice," Cindy promised. She looked up at the sky. "It's getting dark enough for them to start any minute now."

As if she had given a signal, the band launched into "The Star-Spangled Banner." Most of the people seated on the grass got to their feet, and many of them sang the words. When they came to "the rockets' red glare," the fireworks started with a bang.

Out over the still water, from which anchored boats had been cleared earlier in the day, a bomb really did burst in air, with a rat-a-tat-tat of shots, a scream of whistles, and a shower of green and gold streamers. For the next half hour there was no let-up. A Japanese-made shell exploded into a giant chrysanthemum. Another spread branches of color like a weeping willow that reached right down to the water. Tad liked a Niagara Falls display with Roman candles. Cindy preferred a magic fan with gold stars.

Everyone, standing or sitting, had eyes fastened on the fireworks, while the low-lying fog embraced the watchers like a soft cloak. Cindy had the feeling that she and Tad were actually alone, their rough blanket turned into a magic carpet. She wanted to touch him, to make sure he was real, because his pale hair gleaming in the intermittent glow looked like something of which fantasies are made. Instinctively she moved closer, and he put an arm around her. Stroking the hair at the nape of his neck, Cindy said softly, "Tad, while nobody's looking, please kiss me."

Beautiful Banner didn't need her any longer, but she hoped—how she hoped!—that Tad did.